"It's still there between us, Katie," Riley whispered. "Can't you feel it?"

"Yes," she said, the word so soft she barely heard herself. She meant to add that she didn't want to feel whatever was still simmering between them. But she couldn't speak at all when he lifted her hand and placed a kiss in the center of her palm.

"I don't want to rush you, but I do want to kiss you." He held on to both her hand and her gaze. "Can I kiss you?"

Kate knew what her answer should be, but her lips wouldn't form the word. From the moment they'd met, the air around them had been charged with an unseen force that drew them together. The force hadn't lessened.

She cleared her throat and moistened lips that had suddenly gone dry, and let him see her need. "You'd better," she said, and this time her words were strong and clear.

Dear Reader,

I once heard the theory advanced that it was rare for two people in a relationship to love each other equally, that invariably one loved the other more. Interesting. But valid? Kate Marino, the heroine of *Winter Heat*, thinks so. What's more, she's determined not to be that person. However, that's not so easy when her ex-lover moves next door with a yuletide plan to win her back. Love is definitely in the crisp, December air, but how much love is enough?

Wishing you—what else?—love this holiday season. And lots of it!

Happy reading,

Darlene Gardner

P.S. Online readers can visit me at www.darlenegardner.com.

Books by Darlene Gardner

HARLEQUIN TEMPTATION
926—ONE HOT CHANCE
955—COLE FOR CHRISTMAS

HARLEQUIN DUETS
39—FORGET ME? *NOT*
51—THE CUPID CAPER
68—THE HUSBAND HOTEL
77—ANYTHING *YOU* CAN DO…!

DARLENE GARDNER

WINTER HEAT

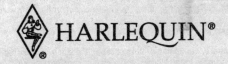

HARLEQUIN®

TORONTO • NEW YORK • LONDON
AMSTERDAM • PARIS • SYDNEY • HAMBURG
STOCKHOLM • ATHENS • TOKYO • MILAN • MADRID
PRAGUE • WARSAW • BUDAPEST • AUCKLAND

To the loves of my life—
Kurt, Paige and Brian—for understanding.

ISBN 0-373-69201-3

WINTER HEAT

Copyright © 2004 by Darlene Hrobak Gardner.

www.eHarlequin.com

Printed in U.S.A.

Prologue

BECAUSE KATE MARINO wanted to hurry down the sidewalk to the quaint Italian restaurant and rush over to Riley Carter's table, she forced herself to slow down.

She window-shopped as she walked past the storefronts lining the narrow street, reminding herself that tourists flocked to Charleston's Market area to peruse the wares of local vendors.

She made herself admire the styling of an off-the-shoulder dress in a vibrant turquoise; stopped to appreciate a painting that boasted bold slashes of crisscrossing color; and bid a merry Christmas to a fat man dressed in a Santa suit.

The anticipation that danced through her at the prospect of meeting Riley, she ignored. Or tried to.

He was just a man, like any other.

A delicious, six-foot package of a man who knew how to make love to her until her brain short-circuited and she could barely think about anything but pleasure.

She shook her head a little, trying to physically clear the images of slick, naked flesh and long, steamy nights.

But her body still tingled with remembered sensations, and she could barely wait to sit down to dinner so they could get the meal over with and start on the more sensual second course.

How had this happened? she wondered as she continued to walk toward the restaurant, this time at her more customary brisk pace.

How had she let herself not only want, but need, a man this way? She, who had vowed never to love until she was positive she had a man's heart in the palm of her hand.

The tiny, white lights that drew attention to the charming restaurant sparkled, like the anticipation inside her. It was all the sweeter because she hadn't thought she'd see Riley tonight.

He'd called early that afternoon to say he needed to work late, but she'd gotten word as she left her own office that his plans had changed. Elle Dumont, a co-worker at her interior design firm, told her Riley had called and asked that Kate meet him for dinner at eight.

Kate had been momentarily surprised that Elle, who had once been Riley's girlfriend, would pass on the message. But high school, Kate figured, had been a long time ago.

Kate had gotten to the Market area, in the touristy heart of Charleston, nearly thirty minutes early. Loath to appear too anxious to meet him, she'd killed time by browsing the ritzy shops in the nearby Charleston Place Hotel.

At precisely eight o'clock, trying to control the

way her heart jumped at the prospect of seeing him, she entered the restaurant.

The place was too small to have a hostess stand, but with tables cleverly positioned to make the most of the intimate space. She scanned the diners, attempting for nonchalance as she sought out the dark-eyed, brown-haired man.

She found him almost immediately, even though his back was partially to the entrance. She took a few quick steps toward him before she noticed the blonde sitting kitty-corner at his table.

Kate slowed when she realized the blonde was Elle Dumont; froze when Elle leaned across the table and kissed Riley full on the mouth.

Even as it occurred to her that Elle must have arranged this whole tableau to make trouble, it registered that Riley didn't pull away. Instead, he leaned into the kiss, actively participating. As their lips clung, Kate's heart ripped apart.

"Good evening. Would you like a table for one or are you meeting someone?"

A perky, young waitress with Mediterranean coloring and a menu appeared in front of her. Kate's head shook, both at what she had seen and at the waitress's questions.

"I was just leaving," she managed to say, her eyes still riveted on Elle and Riley and the kiss that had mercifully ended.

Her voice wasn't loud but Riley still turned. Surprise flitted across his features, followed immediately by guilt. Kate turned swiftly away and walked blindly toward the exit.

"Kate, wait," she heard him call after her as he chased her into the night.

She already knew she wouldn't listen to what was sure to be a rational explanation of how Elle had arranged for Kate to witness the kiss.

Not because Kate didn't believe the other woman capable of such sabotage.

But because Riley had kissed her back.

1

"IF THAT DON'T BEAT ALL," the Realtor drawled over the phone line, the South audible in every syllable. "Here's the perfect sublet, but it's in the building where Kate Marino lives."

Riley Carter's body temperature felt as though it had spiked a good twenty degrees. His grip tightened on the receiver of his cordless phone, his fingers inadvertently depressing some of the buttons.

"Riley, are you there?" the Realtor asked. "Can you hear me? Annelise to Riley. Come in."

Riley waited a beat, swallowed and said, "I can hear you just fine now, Annelise. What were you saying?"

"Just that this sublet won't do at all. Would you look at that?"

He pictured the redheaded Realtor examining the listings on her computer screen through the tiny oval lenses of her fashionable wire-rimmed glasses.

"The place isn't only in the same building as Kate, it's next door."

Next door? With only a wall separating his bed from the one he'd shared with Kate last December?

"Let's see what else we have here. Hmm, furnished sublets… Oh, here's something. But it's in Mount Pleasant. That certainly won't do, considering you already have the place on Sullivan's Island."

Riley had met Annelise Manley through Kate, which was why he'd called Annelise and not another Realtor. Even though Annelise and Kate were only casual acquaintances, no other Realtor could get him both an apartment and an update on the ex-girlfriend whose very name still made his blood run hot. He'd planned to bring up Kate before he rang off, but now wouldn't have to.

"The point is not having to drive over the Cooper River bridges at rush hour," Riley said, instead of blurting out that he'd take the apartment in Kate's building. He'd work up to that slowly. "The apartment's got to be in peninsular Charleston."

The long commute had become difficult after an investment group hired his and his brother's design and construction firm to build a luxury hotel in a revitalized section of the city. Riley, an architect who had yet to turn thirty, was aware the project could catapult the business he owned with his brother, Dave, into a new level of success.

"Then you're out of luck," Annelise said. "Furnished sublets are a rare commodity as it is. I'm afraid very few of them become available in December."

December. The month he'd met Kate Marino. And the month he'd foolishly let her go.

"I can keep an eye peeled, but I wouldn't hold

out much hope until after the holidays," Annelise continued.

"Why won't it do?" Riley made sure to keep his voice casual.

"Excuse me?"

"The sublet in Kate's building. Why won't it do?"

A pause came from the other end of the phone line. "Because it seems to me I remember hearing something about you two having a bad breakup."

Riley made a face, glad Annelise couldn't see him. He and Kate had broken up by mutual consent, with neither of them trying very hard to hang on to what they'd had.

At the time, he'd thought their relationship was like an ember that burned hot and bright but couldn't withstand a cold gust of reality.

He usually made it a point to get to know a woman before he slept with her. But he hadn't known much more about Kate than her name when they'd wound up in bed together just hours after first laying eyes on each other.

That their relationship had imploded hadn't been a surprise—not when he'd gone against his slow, deliberate nature to embrace the fast and the furious. But here it was a year later, and he couldn't stop thinking about Kate.

Even before he'd called Annelise, he'd been mulling over ways to insinuate himself back into Kate's life. He'd known he would have to take things slowly this time, but, at best, his plan had been half formed.

"I wouldn't call it a bad breakup," he hedged.

Riley stopped himself before adding that he and Kate were still friends. The truth was, they'd never been friends. They'd become lovers so quickly, they'd gotten to know each other better in bed than out of it. That had been the crux of the problem.

"Oh, really? Maybe I have my information wrong then. I thought I heard…" Annelise's voice tailed off, then started up again. "Aren't you dating that woman who used to work in her office?"

Riley covered the receiver so she wouldn't hear him sigh. He paced to the screen door of his house, which was only a few blocks from the ocean, and let the salty breeze wash over him. The rumor mill had been busy, but he doubted it had been kind.

Until six months ago Kate worked for the same interior design firm as Elle Dumont, who had grown up a few blocks from his family in the historic, old-money section of Charleston.

When Kate had come across Elle kissing him, she hadn't given him the benefit of the doubt. To be fair, he hadn't put much effort into convincing Kate the kiss meant nothing. Guilt over kissing Elle back had handcuffed him.

"Elle and I haven't dated since high school." Riley refrained from adding that their mothers were best friends who'd pushed them together then, and hadn't given up trying. "I'm not dating anybody."

"Interesting," Annelise said. "Last I heard, Kate was dating a lot."

Damn. But what had he expected? Any claim he

had on Kate had ended with their relationship. But if she wasn't married, or engaged, he still had a chance.

"Good for her," Riley said through clenched teeth. "Now, about that sublet. How soon can I have it?"

"You haven't even seen it."

"Circa 1800s house, built in the Victorian style. South of Broad, in the Historic District. Subdivided into four apartments on three floors before the Historic Charleston Foundation came into prominence. Sound about right?"

"You described the building, not the apartment."

"I'm not picky. I need an apartment near the construction site, and it's the only one available," Riley said, which was the truth. Annelise didn't need to know that his primary reason for wanting an apartment had become secondary during their conversation. "I'm sure it will be fine."

"I don't know," Annelise wavered. "Maybe I should call Kate, see what she has to say."

"Kate will say it's no big deal, the same as me," Riley bluffed. He actually had a pretty good idea that Kate wouldn't be thrilled to find him living next door. "Come on, Annelise. I really need this place."

"Okay," Annelise said after a moment. "Give me a deposit, I'll get you a key and you can move in this weekend."

Her timetable made sense. It had been what he'd hoped she would suggest. Still, he found himself saying, "It's only Tuesday, Annelise. Why can't I move in tomorrow?"

"Well, I suppose you could…"

"Then I will. I'll pick up the key in the morning," Riley said, then hung up and made a note to himself in his PalmPilot.

The plan to win Kate back was now fully formed. Who would have guessed his chance to implement it would come in the form of a gift-wrapped apartment?

IF THERE WERE A HELL, the devil probably forced all the single, doomed souls inhabiting it to go on dates.

Not those rare I-can't-believe-I've-found-you kind of dates. Bad dates. The kind marked by awkward silences, stilted conversation and zero sexual chemistry.

The only kind Kate Marino had known since reentering the dating world four men ago. The kind that was coming to a merciful end with man number five.

She hurried up the interior stairway to her apartment, unable to gain ground on the trailing Drew Lockhart no matter how fast she went. She'd tried a quick goodbye wave from the head of the porch, but it hadn't gotten rid of him.

At the top of the stairs, she rounded the corner at warp speed and navigated the short hallway, her apartment key already in hand. But before she could unlock the door, Drew managed to catch up.

"You must have run track in high school. I could barely keep up." He sounded slightly out of breath, which she hoped was only because of their mad dash up the stairs.

"Nope." Kate fiddled with her key in the lock. *Turn already*, she thought. "I was a cheerleader. You know—give me a G-O-O-D-N-I-G-H-T. Good night!"

He smiled, making Kate understand why other women considered him a heartbreaker. His blue eyes and pale complexion presented a striking complement to his curly, ink-black hair. His pedigree was top-notch, too. He hailed from a fine Charleston family that contributed heavily to the arts. Drew himself was a concert violinist.

"I like you," he said. "You're funny."

Kate shut her mouth. She did not want to be funny.

"I had a nice time tonight," he continued.

She narrowed her eyes. Hadn't he noticed that they'd failed to find a topic of mutual interest? He'd changed the subject every time she mentioned interior design, and her eyes had glazed over when he opined about which of Beethoven's sonatas were superior.

"I'd like to see you again." Drew flattened his palm against her apartment door and leaned over her. The cloying scent of cologne engulfed her. "How about Saturday night?"

Before she could refuse, his head descended, his mouth leading the way. His sudden motion blocked the light, causing everything to turn black. Without thinking, Kate lifted her foot and connected with his instep.

"Ow!" he cried out, jumping back a full foot. "What did you do that for?"

"Well, it was just…that I… Did it occur to you I might not want you to kiss me?" she sputtered.

"Did it occur to you to tell me to stop?" His pretty blue eyes watered. "You didn't have to resort to violence."

"Stepping on a foot isn't exactly assault and battery."

He didn't respond, and the remorse that had been slow in coming finally arrived. With his pout and his unhappy eyes, he looked as harmless as a puppy. She grimaced. Bad date or not, how could she have gone on the attack like that?

"I'm sorry," Kate said, trying for sincerity. Drew stared, his lower lip thrust forward in a pout.

"I'm *really* sorry," she said. "How can I make it up to you?"

He pressed his lips together, and she heard him blow air out through his nose. "I'd suggest an assault-free date, but I'm not taking any more chances. Tell you what—if you decide you want to see me again, you call me."

He disappeared down the hallway, limping slightly, his right hand raised in a harmless salute. She frowned, aware she may have overreacted.

Drew paused at the mouth of the staircase. She tensed, ready to overreact again if he reversed course. But he merely moved aside, as though allowing someone to pass.

That was odd. Kate hadn't heard footsteps on the wooden stairs, and the owner of the only other apartment on this floor was a salesman on extended assignment to the west coast.

Curious, Kate waited. The hallway passage was

softly lit, so she was slow in recognizing the features of the man who walked toward her. She squinted.

Could it be... Riley Carter?

For an instant, she thought she'd dredged him up from her subconscious, where he'd been lurking more than usual since December had rolled around again. But she couldn't mistake his self-assured, unhurried way of moving. Or his tall, muscular frame. Or that thick head of brown hair.

It *was* Riley Carter.

Her heart pounded. He had to be here because of her. Nobody else lived on this floor, and it was nearly ten o'clock on a Wednesday night.

Heat started to flood her body, the way it used to whenever he came anywhere near. But then she remembered all the days and nights she'd waited in vain for him to show up and beg her forgiveness.

A year ago, she'd have welcomed him into her apartment—and her bed—no matter what time he showed up. Eleven months ago, he probably could have convinced her to take him back.

But his window of opportunity had closed a long time ago. It might have taken her a while to get over him, but she had. She wouldn't let the bittersweet memories of the long, hot nights they'd shared last December ruin this year's holidays. She was dating again. She was happy.

She stiffened her spine, crossed her arms over her chest and resolved not to be affected by the sexual chemistry that had always flared so brightly between them.

"Hey, Kate, how's it going?" He sounded as though he'd seen her only yesterday.

She told herself she didn't find his slow, southern drawl sexy, and willed her voice to sound cool. "Are you familiar with the saying, 'Too little, too late'?"

He rubbed his chin as he considered her. It was a nice chin, square and regular. Taken individually, none of his features—lean cheeks, straight nose, firm mouth, light brown hair, dark brown eyes—were outstanding. Put together, they packed a visual punch that used to make her legs go weak. She locked her knees.

"Yeah," he said, finally. "I am familiar with it."

"Then it won't come as any surprise to you that I've moved on."

He cocked his head, a corner of his well-shaped mouth lifting. "I thought you still lived here."

"Not moved," Kate said impatiently. "Moved *on*. As in, moved on to other men."

"Okay."

She lifted her chin, ignoring the part of her that was disappointed he hadn't cried out in protest. "You probably passed one of the men I'm dating on the stairs."

"The limping guy?"

His eyes were round and innocent, but she couldn't shake the impression that he'd heard what had gone on between her and Drew. Great. Just great.

"Drew is only one of the men I'm dating," she said airily. "There are others."

"Good for you."

He smiled at her then, causing the laugh lines around his mouth and eyes to deepen. He looked so attractive, her patience snapped. She wouldn't let herself fall for him again.

"Look, it's late and I'm tired." She got her door unlocked, pushed it open and stepped partway inside her apartment. "You wasted your time coming over here."

"Oh, I wouldn't say that," he said in a low drawl that rumbled through her.

"I *did* say that," she said, just to be contrary. "Good night, Riley."

"Good night, Kate," he said agreeably, not even trying to stop her from going inside. Not that he could.

She was about to shut the door in his face when she noticed him take something that jingled out of his pocket.

His key ring.

She felt her mouth drop open as he used one of the keys to unlock the apartment next door.

"What are you doing?" she asked, although she feared she already knew.

"Subletting the apartment next door," he said with a wink. "'Night, neighbor."

LESS THAN TEN HOURS after he'd seen Kate Marino again, Riley already craved another look at her.

Her dark hair had been long and straight when they'd dated, but now it was cut in short, flyaway layers that emphasized her large, nut-brown eyes and olive skin. With her coltish, long-legged frame and sassy way of dressing, she'd reminded him of an Italian Meg Ryan the first time he'd seen her.

But now she was just Kate, plain and simple.

The next time he saw her he'd prefer she not be scowling at him, the way she had last night. But he could be patient. If his plan worked, he'd not only win her heart, but the right to her bed, as well.

He remembered the way her body felt against his, slick skin sliding against slick skin, as they—

A flash of red penetrated his daydream, and he slammed on the brakes of his SUV so he didn't run the red light. He craned his neck and looked over his shoulder, the sun at his back almost blinding him.

Damn. He'd driven by the construction site.

When the light glowed green, he carefully turned the SUV around, parked and got out. His accelerated heartbeat might be due to the constantly evolving building that was to become the Hotel Charleston, but he wouldn't put money on it.

Still, watching his vision take shape and form was a powerful high.

Today, the crane stood motionless beside the steel skeleton of the building. But Riley imagined five stories of brick and mortar, harkening to the days when horses roamed the streets and men in red coats were the enemy.

Deliberately turning his mind away from Kate and toward business, he walked along the edge of the construction site to a metallic trailer that glowed silver in the weak sunlight and climbed the three steps to the open door.

His business partner, who doubled as his brother, sat at a rickety desk while biting into a chocolate-glazed donut.

"'Morning, Dave," Riley said. "Did you save one of those donuts for me?"

"Now is not the time to bum one of my donuts," Dave growled without glancing up from the papers spread in front of him.

Riley lowered himself into a nearby chair as he studied his brother, who washed the donut down with coffee. Extra cream. Two sugars.

Their family resemblance was uncanny, especially around the mouth and jaw, but Dave was a pumped up version of Riley. Older by five years and larger by about five percent, he had washboard abs, impressive musculature and low body fat despite his fondness for junk food.

Riley didn't have to wait long for his brother to tell him what was wrong.

"Damn it." Dave pounded the desk so hard, it rattled and the papers shifted. "We have to scrap the marble flooring in the lobby."

"No, we don't," Riley said calmly.

"I got three quotes that say we do." Dave shoved back his chair, stood and paced from one end of the trailer to the other in four steps. He gestured jerkily at the papers. "Check it out yourself."

Riley walked to the desk, picked up the paper-work and examined the individual sheets before setting them down. "You got three unreasonable quotes, is what you got."

"Don't you get it? They're all within a couple hundred dollars," Dave raged. "We can't go over budget on the flooring, not after the electrical work cost more than we figured. We can't do the marble. We just can't."

"We will," Riley said, sitting back down. "I know a couple places we can check in Berkeley County that might be more reasonable."

"And if they're not?" Dave shot at him.

"Then we'll deal with that when we get there."

Dave rubbed the back of his neck as he directed his scowl at Riley. "It really bugs me how you do that."

"Do what?"

"Keep your cool."

"Next time, I can cuss and wave my hands if it'll make you feel better."

"Nah. I do enough of that for both of us. Hell, Riley, aren't you worried at all?"

"Why should I be?" Riley crossed his legs at the ankles and linked his hands behind his neck. "We're damn good at what we do. When we're done with this hotel, everybody will know that."

"But this job can make or break us."

"I told you when we went into business together that we'd get a major job by this point. It was part of the five-year plan. We're ready for it."

"Easy for you to say," Dave groused. "You always were a methodical bastard."

Darlene Gardner   23

"Thanks," Riley said.

Dave propped himself up on the edge of the desk and pointed the ink end of a pen at Riley. "You're irritating, did you know that?"

"Yep."

Dave narrowed his eyes. "What are you doing here so early, anyway? What gives? No traffic on the bridge?"

"I didn't drive the bridge this morning," Riley said.

His house on Sullivan's Island was about twelve miles from peninsular Charleston, but the drive took the better part of an hour if traffic was heavy on the twin spans that towered over the Cooper River.

"Well, hallelujah," Dave said. "It's about time you found another woman."

"I found an apartment so I can stay in town during the week," Riley corrected. "Although, if you want, we could refer to it as a 'she,' like a boat."

"An apartment where?"

"On Ashley Avenue near Tradd."

Dave's thick, dark eyebrows drew together. "Ashley Avenue. Now why does it seem to me you know somebody on Ashley?"

Riley took his time in answering. "Kate Marino lives on Ashley."

"The woman who dumped you last Christmas?"

"That's the one," Riley agreed.

"And now you're living with her?"

"Not with her. Next door. I needed a sublet, and the place next to hers was available."

"You're saying that was a coincidence?"

"Yep."

"Come off it, squirt." Dave used his childhood nickname for Riley, who'd been undersized until his teens. "You're not living there by chance. You don't do anything without a blueprint."

Riley figured he might as well give it up. Keeping secrets from his brother never worked anyway.

"It was more an opportunity than a coincidence," he confessed. "I figure it's a chance to get her back."

Dave snorted. "This is not a good idea, little brother."

"Why not?"

"Not five minutes ago, you agreed this project was major for us. Yesterday, you were talking about putting extra time in to make sure the proposal for the next job was perfect."

"Man cannot live on work alone."

"Neither can he afford to waste his time on a woman who won't take him back."

"How do you know she won't take me back?"

"I know a lot of things."

"Yeah, like how to keep from committing to the women you sleep with."

"I know enough to call it quits when it's over." Dave hopped off the desk. "This woman already dumped you once, kid. What makes you think it'll be any different this time?"

"Because this time, I'm not going to sleep with her," Riley stated. "Not until I make friends with her first."

Dave threw back his head and laughed, long and loud.

"I'm not sure why, yet," Riley said, "but I'm pretty sure I resent that laugh."

"Squirt, you spent last December practically living at this woman's apartment. If she lets you anywhere near her, you won't be able to keep your hands off her."

"Will, too."

Dave snagged the last donut before he headed for the exit. "Dream on, little brother," he called. "Dream on."

2

THE HEELS OF KATE'S funky purple shoes made rapid clicking sounds on the lacquered wood floor of the Designs on You office. She nodded at the receptionist sitting at the holly-draped desk as she went by.

"Not so fast, Kate." The receptionist waved some message slips at her that came off a memo pad featuring flying reindeer pulling Santa's sleigh. "You must be doing something right, because people want you."

"Thanks." Kate paused to smile at the sweet-faced, middle-aged woman before she walked off, flipping through the messages as she went. Two from clients, one from her mother, one from a guy she'd met in the grocery store last week. None from Riley. She called back over her shoulder, "Too bad only one of the people who want me is an eligible man."

The receptionist's laughter followed her as she continued to her private office and closed the door.

She did a quick perusal of her office, her chest falling in relief when she located the fabric samples she needed for her two o'clock meeting.

She checked the time on the triangular wall clock that she'd found in a trendy little shop the last time she'd been in New York City. Doing some quick calculations, she figured she had thirty schedule-free minutes before she needed to leave for her appointment.

She peeled off the long, wool-blend jacket she'd paired with a lipstick-red turtleneck and matching flare-leg slacks, and collapsed into the upholstered chair behind her desk.

No wonder she'd forgotten the samples. She'd been on the go since nine that morning, picking out furniture, checking out interiors and meeting with clients.

She'd done it all on a short night's sleep, because she'd lain awake half the night trying to figure out whether Riley Carter had moved next door to her for a reason.

She thumbed through the Christmas-themed message slips, just in case she'd missed Riley's name the first time around. Nope. Nothing.

Then she tapped her mother's message against her palm. She should return the call, but she'd do it later. Her brother had already e-mailed to tell her Dad was out of work again, and Kate wasn't in the mood to listen to Mom make excuses for him.

She put that message slip aside and picked up another. This one was from the dentist who'd banged his cart into hers at the grocery store.

He'd flashed her an exceedingly white smile, apologized for a collision that hadn't been accidental and asked for her phone number.

Giving him her office number had seemed like a good idea at the time, but at the moment, going out with the dentist had as much appeal as a shot of Novocain.

She picked up the phone to call him with her regrets but three quick raps interrupted her before she could dial. The door opened a crack, and Elle Dumont stuck her beautiful, blond head into the office.

"Oh, good, you're here. You don't mind if I come in, do you?" Without waiting for an answer, Elle opened the door the rest of the way and breezed in, looking like she'd stepped out of the pages of *Southern Living* magazine.

Elle had been first runner-up in the Miss South Carolina pageant a few years back, which she mentioned with regularity in casual conversation. She wore her golden blond hair long and loose around her shoulders, her dress snug around the bodice and her southernism so blatantly, Kate wouldn't be surprised if she started whistling Dixie.

"Good afternoon, Elle," Kate said tightly, and set the phone back down on its cradle. "Did I miss something, or are you working here again?"

"Of course not, silly. Peter couldn't begin to pay me what I'm making over at Dixie Kane Interiors," Elle said, referring to Kate's boss. She wore three-inch heels but seemed to float when she approached the desk. "He's such a dear to understand I'd outgrown this place and needed to move on. I stopped by to tell him hello and thought I'd pop in to see you, too."

Kate felt the skin of her face stretch as she resisted the urge to bare her teeth. "I hadn't realized we were on a pop-in basis."

Elle placed her hands on hips that probably measured a perfect twelve inches more than her waist. The corners of her salmon-tinged lips lifted in a closed-mouth smile.

"We were co-workers for six months, Kate. Of course I want to catch up. Especially since Peter told me your idea to branch out into hospitality design. You are so brave to even think about going up against the big boys."

Kate set her teeth, fully aware that Elle's employer was the biggest of the big boys. "The largest firm isn't always the best choice for a project."

"Maybe not, but it might be tough going for you for a while. One thing I've learned at Dixie Kane is that competition for these jobs is fierce. Let's hope the clients don't overlook those quirky little residential interiors you're so wonderful at designing."

Elle's thinly veiled jab was a reminder that Kate was a designer who preferred the unusual in a city wedded to the past. Kate closed her eyes, counted to three and made a wish that wasn't granted. Because when she opened them, Elle was still there. "So you came in here to offer me your support?"

Elle gave a pretty, little sigh that sounded like she practiced it. "That's not the only reason. I wanted to make sure things between us weren't awkward seeing as how we're sure to be bumping into each other more often."

"Why is that?"

Elle placed her beautifully manicured nails on her chest. "Because Riley's living next door to you, of course."

Kate fought to keep her features impassive, although her insides felt as though they were crumbling.

"I know you and I have never been friends," Elle said, batting her long, mascaraed lashes in a pantomime of innocence, "but I don't fancy having you for an enemy."

"I hate to break this to you, Elle, but I don't think about you enough to consider you either."

"What a relief. But you have to admit, it is uncomfortable. It would have been so much better if Riley had stayed put on Sullivan's Island. Not that he had a choice, with the hotel in the mix, and all."

Kate swallowed but couldn't stop her question. "What hotel?"

"Why, the Hotel Charleston." Elle's large, green eyes went wide. "The big, fancy place over by the aquarium. Riley wouldn't be needing a place in town if he wasn't overseeing construction."

Of course. The hotel Riley had been designing last year when they were together. Kate knew about it—had even driven out of her way several times to check on its progress—but it hadn't occurred to her as the reason he'd moved into her apartment building.

She'd preferred to think it was because he wanted her back. How stupid that had been. Especially because he hadn't tried very hard to hang on to her in the first place.

"So you can see why I'm concerned," Elle finished.

"No," Kate said. "I can't."

"Oh, come on, Kate." Elle stepped closer, so that her flowery scent engulfed Kate. It took all Kate's restraint not to blow air deliberately out her nose. "You haven't exactly been warm and fuzzy toward me since the restaurant incident."

Kate caught the tip of her tongue between her teeth so she wouldn't call Elle an unflattering name. After she'd gotten over her initial shock, she'd never doubted that Elle had arranged for her to witness the kiss.

Riley's story bore that out. He claimed Elle had asked him to dinner to talk about a family problem, and that she'd been the one to reach across the table and kiss him.

But he'd never explained why he'd kissed her back.

"I'm so glad we cleared the air between us." Elle bestowed Kate with another smile that seemed sincere but wasn't. "It'll make things so much easier for all three of us."

"Would you do something for me, Elle?" Kate asked.

"Sure."

"Shut the door on your way out."

Elle's smile faltered but she resurrected it before nodding and leaving the office. Kate kneaded her forehead, trying to hold off a headache. Elle hadn't meant anything good by her little visit, but it had served as a useful purpose.

It reminded Kate how lopsided her affair with Riley had been. She was the one who'd asked him to walk her home the night they'd met. She'd invited him into her apartment and her bed. She'd allowed herself to become so crazy about him that she hadn't wanted to date anyone else.

All the time they were seeing each other, she'd wondered if he felt the same way. When she'd seen him with Elle, she had her answer. But after all this time, a part of her still wanted the answer to be different.

But what if Elle was just making trouble again? What if Riley had moved in next door because of her?

She quickly dialed her friend, Annelise Manley, who'd been the listing agent on the apartment next door, to find out. Afterward, she sat frozen in her chair, the knowledge that Riley had gotten the place next door by chance burning like acid.

He'd told Annelise not to worry about them being neighbors because it was no big deal.

No big deal.

She pressed her lips together. She wasn't a fool. She'd felt the current running hot and heavy between them last night and knew Riley had felt it, too. Proximity would make it only too easy to fall back into bed with him—unless she made it perfectly clear that she was unavailable.

"Fool me once, shame on you," she said aloud as

she picked up the phone and punched in a number. "Fool me twice…well, that's not happening."

"Hello," a deep, male voice said a moment later.

"Dennis? It's Kate Marino returning your call. Of course I remember meeting you at the grocery store. And I'd love to go out with you."

HOLDING HIS BLACK leather briefcase in one hand and a bag of Chinese takeout in the other, Riley used his hip to close the door of his SUV before starting up the sidewalk to his temporary home.

The house was only blocks from the southernmost tip of the peninsula, and a cool, salty breeze blew in from the direction of the Charleston harbor. The wind seemed to cut through his pant legs, but he took his time while he contemplated his next move.

Kate's electric-green Toyota MR2 Spyder was parked on the street, but he doubted she'd had time to fix dinner yet. She hadn't gotten home from work last night until seven, and it was only half past six now.

An invitation to share his wonton soup, shrimp egg rolls and kung pao chicken would strike exactly the right note. Neighborly. Friendly. So how could he make it an offer she couldn't refuse?

He noticed as he came up the outside stairs that his downstairs neighbors had adorned the porch with large poinsettias, providing vibrant splashes of red against the backdrop of the house's pale yellow siding.

The poinsettias reminded him of last Christmas

with Kate, so she seemed almost an apparition when she appeared in front of him. The attraction that jolted him was real enough, and so powerful he almost dropped the food.

He'd never been drawn to a particular type of woman before but now knew exactly what he preferred. An average-height, medium-weight brunette, her hair cut to look artfully messy, her eyes as dark as bittersweet chocolate. She was dressed stylishly in low-waisted, flared jeans and a red leather jacket that ended where her belt line began. A red, newsboy cap and a striped scarf completed the very appealing picture.

He couldn't have stopped his smile any more than he could quit designing buildings. He climbed the remaining few steps to the porch with a new spring in his step.

"Hey, Kate," he said at the same moment a man with a big nose and a wispy mustache followed her onto the porch. Riley disliked him on sight, even before the man put a proprietary hand at her back.

"Riley," she said, nodding and moving to get past him.

He stepped sideways to block her, careful not to let his smile slip. Since she'd had a date Wednesday night, and tonight was Friday, he probably should have figured she'd have another. But what the hell was she doing with this character? *Be friendly*, he warned himself. "Nice evening, isn't it?"

The breeze blowing off the harbor gusted, sweeping over the porch and making Kate hold on to her cap. She shivered.

"I mean, it's a nice evening if you like a cold, damp wind," Riley continued, then added lamely, "which I do."

Kate was silent, but her eyes shifted, as though she were plotting to get around him. But how could he get this guy's hand off her back? With a stroke of inspiration, he put down his briefcase and stuck his right hand out to the mustache-challenged guy.

"I'm Riley Carter."

"Dennis McElroy." The man dropped his hand from Kate's back to make it available for shaking. His teeth were so blindingly white that Riley blinked to protect his eyes from the glare. But his grip was weak. Good.

"*Dr.* Dennis McElroy," Kate clarified.

The wind howled, drowning out part of what Dennis said next, but it sounded like, "I'm a Dennis."

How do you respond to something like that? "I'm a Riley," he said.

"No, no. I said I was a *dentist.*"

Under other circumstances, Riley would have difficulty taking Dennis the dentist seriously. But he couldn't underestimate any guy who'd gotten a date with Kate.

"I'm an architect." Riley watched with displeasure as Dennis's hand returned to Kate's back. "Kate and I used to go out."

Dennis's hand plummeted until it was back at his side. The dentist blinked rapidly a few times. "Are you here to see Kate?"

"No, he's not," Kate answered before he could. "Riley lives here."

A soft cry of dismay escaped from beneath Dennis's flimsy mustache. "I didn't realize you were living with anybody, Kate."

Kate shook her head. "Riley doesn't live *with* me. He lives next door."

"Couldn't ask for a better neighbor." Riley slanted Kate a long, appreciative look. "Or a prettier one."

Confusion settled over Dennis's features. Bingo.

"Riley isn't living here because of me, Dennis." Kate sent Riley a withering glare. "He's supervising the construction of a hotel that's going up near the aquarium and needed a place in the city for a few months."

"How do you know that?" Riley asked. "I don't remember mentioning it."

Kate lifted her chin. "Your girlfriend told me."

"My girlfriend? Now who would that be?"

"That," she said with what he recognized as false sweetness, "would be Elle."

He forced himself to laugh even though this wasn't funny. It reminded him too vividly of last December, and the gulf that had sprung between them after that stupid kiss he'd shared with Elle.

"Elle hasn't been my girlfriend since high school."

"Then how does she know you're living here?"

"I expect she heard it from her mother. You do remember that my mother and Elle's mother are friends."

"I've never met your mother. And we were over so long ago, I can't be expected to remember much about you."

"I remember lots about you," he said, keeping his voice light and friendly, "including that you have a good memory."

Somebody cleared his throat, and Riley realized he'd nearly forgotten Dennis. "We have reservations for seven o'clock, Kate," he said.

"Where are you going?" Riley asked conversationally.

"That's none of your—" Kate said at the same time Dennis answered, "Garibaldi's."

"Nice place. Kate and I went there on our first date."

"No, we didn't. We went to 82 Queen."

"You're right, we did." Riley winked at her. "Good memory."

Kate stared at him speechlessly while Dennis shifted his weight from his right foot to his left. Riley thought about asking Dennis if he specialized in any specific kind of dental work, but he only had so much friendliness in him.

"Don't let me keep you." Riley picked up his briefcase and stepped around them. "They won't hold that reservation forever."

KATE PAUSED AT THE TOP of the stairs and stole a look down the hallway. When she determined all was clear, she hurried to her apartment and didn't relax until she was locked inside.

She couldn't deal with Riley, not after that weird encounter on the front porch earlier that evening. She couldn't fathom what he'd been trying to accomplish, but things with Dennis had gone quickly downhill soon after he'd left them.

A shrill ringing interrupted the quiet. She startled, then felt silly when she realized the sound had come from the phone. Hurrying into her kitchen, she snatched up the receiver and said hello.

"Kate, dear, it's your mother."

Warmth flowed through Kate at the sound of her mother's familiar voice, followed quickly by guilt. "Mom. Hi. I'm sorry I didn't return your call. The past couple days have been crazy."

"Does that have anything to do with your old boss wanting you back? Because it would be lovely to have you back in Philadelphia."

The hope in her mother's voice made Kate wince. She shouldn't have told her mother about last week's phone call, especially because she wasn't seriously considering leaving Designs on You.

"I haven't given it much thought," Kate said. "I'm happy here in Charleston. You know that."

"Maybe so, but it never hurts to listen to someone who wants to give you a job. Good ones are hard to find. Ask your father."

Kate felt her body tense. It hadn't taken Mom long to get to the point of the phone call. "Johnny e-mailed me about him being fired."

"Did your brother also tell you his supervisor had it in for him? The writing was on the wall last month when he accused your dad of padding his expense account. Can you imagine! As though your father would do such a thing."

Kate could well imagine him doing much worse.
But her mother's love for her father was so all-con-
suming, she didn't feel hot air blast her every time
Dad opened his mouth.

Kate swallowed both her opinion and her
exasperation. "What's he going to do now?"

"Find another job, of course. You know how con-
scientious and hardworking he is. The trick is finding something worthy of him. He's overqualified for
so many jobs."

Kate dutifully listened while her mother spewed
more nonsense that must have come straight from
Dad. When Kate had been a little girl, she'd thought
Dad hung the moon, too. But she'd grown up and
recognized him for the empty charmer he was. Her
stable, hardworking mother, who'd kept food on the
table and a roof over their heads, still didn't see it.

"Yeah, right," she muttered after she'd finally put
the receiver back on the cradle. "If Dad were half the
salesman Mom thinks he is, he'd succeed in selling
something other than garbage."

Although fatigue weighed down her limbs and
pulled at her eyelids, her mind was restless. Outside,
the half moon peeked through the clouds and shed
a faint light through her French door, beckoning her
onto the balcony.

She pulled on her leather jacket and stepped into
the night. Cloud cover had prevented the temperature
from dipping too low, and the night felt more refreshing than frosty now that the wind had died down.

She shoved her mother's exasperating gullibility

from her mind, but that brought this evening's date with the solicitous Dennis to the forefront.

He'd made the dinner reservation for Garibaldi's but would have cheerfully gone somewhere else if she'd rather. If she were cold, he'd turn on his car heater. He'd prefer not to eat dessert but would if she wanted to indulge.

She'd tried to enjoy herself, even suggesting a place for after-dinner drinks when Dennis insisted she choose, but couldn't wait to be free of him.

"That," she said aloud, "was awful."

"So the date was a bust, then?"

Riley's soft drawl interrupted the quiet of the night. She whirled. He sat in a rocking chair not more than ten feet from her on the narrow wraparound balcony their apartments shared.

"What are you doing out here?" she asked.

"Enjoying the night. Same as you, I expect." He rose, limb by long limb, and stretched. He seemed to fill the night, his presence so overpowering that she gripped the handrail to keep strong.

"Even if I do accept that you like the cold and the damp," she said with undisguised skepticism, "it's hard to believe you sit outside on December nights appreciating them."

His deep laugh rumbled through her, as unsettling as an earthquake. "You got me. I didn't come out here until I heard you come home."

"How did you know I'd come outside?"

"I didn't. I was waiting until you got off the phone to knock on your balcony door."

Her heart dropped what felt like a foot. Did he intend to convince her to let him share her bed again?

"Why would you do that?" She meant to sound chilly, but her voice came out strangled.

He crossed the balcony, coming close enough to blot out what she could see of the moon. His face was in shadows, but her memory filled in what was too tough to see.

Eyes that crinkled at the corners and a nose that dipped at the tip. A jaw darkened by a day's growth of beard, so that it would feel raspy against her face. A top lip that curved sensuously over the lower one.

Her heart thudded, her palms grew damp and her breathing hitched, her senses reacting the way they used to a year ago whenever he came near. He didn't touch her, but she felt him all the same.

"I thought you might want to tell me about your date with Dennis the dentist," he said quietly.

She swallowed, and prayed he wouldn't guess her mind had been on sex when his was on Dennis. She straightened her spine. "Why would I want to tell you anything about Dennis?"

"I thought women liked to talk about these things."

"Not to their ex-boyfriends!"

"Then pretend I'm someone else."

"I can't do that," she protested.

He shrugged shoulders that looked even broader in the heavy canvas shirt he wore over his pullover. "Try me. I'm a good listener."

This was as strange as the conversation on the front porch had been. "It was a terrific date," she lied.

"Terrific, huh?" Riley scratched his head. "That's not what you said a minute ago. You said it was awful."

"Do you make a habit of eavesdropping on me?"

"I don't think you can call it eavesdropping when somebody's talking to themselves."

"Maybe I was referring to my mother's phone call instead of the date," she bluffed.

"You don't get along with your mother?"

"Of course I do. I love her."

"Then why is talking to her on the phone so awful?"

"I don't want to have this discussion with you," she said, then could have kicked herself for confirming there was something to discuss.

"Then tell me about the date."

"I had a very nice time," she snapped. "Dennis is very…accommodating."

"You mean he's a yes-man?" Riley stroked his chin. "I got a hint of that, too. So is that what got on your nerves? Is he too meek for you?"

"First you eavesdrop, now you're not listening. I said I had a nice time."

"If that's true," he said, seeming to imply that it wasn't, "then I'm glad."

"You're glad?" She shook her head, closed her eyes, put two fingers to each of her temples. "I don't understand what you're doing, Riley."

"What do you mean?"

"First the twenty questions on the front porch, now this post-date interrogation." She snapped her eyes open. "What gives?"

"Just being friendly."

"Friendly?"

"Yeah," he said and shrugged. "I figured that you and me, we could be friends."

"Friends!" She was aware that she was parroting him, but what he was saying was preposterous. "We can't be friends."

"Why not?" He sounded vaguely insulted. "I make a good friend."

"Riley, we spent all of last December in bed."

One of his dark eyebrows lifted. "I know. I was there. But being lovers didn't work out so great."

She felt the flush start at her neck and advance northward. Did he think she was propositioning him? "I wasn't suggesting we be lovers."

"That's why we should try the friend thing."

She expelled a disbelieving breath. "I think we should stay away from each other."

"Pretty hard to do considering we're next-door neighbors."

"But not impossible." She pointed a finger at him. "We could do it if we tried."

"Don't trust yourself around me, do you?"

He took a step toward her, and the night grew instantly warmer. Her gaze dipped to his mouth. Of all his features, she'd always loved his mouth the best. It could be either incredibly soft or breathlessly demanding. Now it was smiling.

He was teasing her. *Teasing her.*

"That's a ridiculous thing to say," she said tightly, preferring to attribute her elevated body temperature to temper.

"Then it's settled." He rocked back on his heels. "We'll keep it strictly friendly."

He dropped a kiss on her nose—on her nose!—before turning and disappearing inside his apartment.

She stood in the darkness, wondering how he'd gotten her to agree to his ridiculous suggestion while she wished for one of those stiff breezes off the harbor to cool her down.

3

THINK FRIENDLY THOUGHTS.

The strategy firmly in mind, Riley rapped on the heavy wooden door to Kate's apartment. Because she'd probably check the peephole before opening it, he arranged his features into what he hoped was a pleasant, non-lascivious expression. The kind a friend knocking on your door on a Saturday morning might wear.

As the seconds ticked by, he tried very hard to shut out the wet, sleek image he'd gotten of her when he'd heard her shower running this morning.

Friendly thoughts.

He was about to knock again when the door opened a crack not much more than six inches wide. He got a good enough look at Kate through the opening to get his blood pumping.

Her damp hair curled around a face free of makeup. A thick, red robe covered her, but he well remembered what every inch of her body looked like.

He locked eyes with her, fighting the urge to let his gaze dip to the tantalizing glimpse of cleavage the robe's V neckline afforded. Damn, was she naked under there?

Her eyes flashed, and for a second he thought she'd intercepted the naked thought, but then she asked, "Do you have any idea what time it is?"

He checked his watch. "Almost eight-thirty."

"Eight-thirty on a *Saturday* morning." She emphasized the day of the week. "You're not supposed to knock on doors this early."

"Why not?"

"People sleep in on Saturdays."

"You didn't. You've been awake for at least forty-five minutes. I heard you in the shower."

He'd made love to her in that shower on more than one steamy occasion last December, but he couldn't think about that right now.

A flash of remembrance seemed to cross her face, but then it was gone. "That doesn't mean I want visitors," she said tightly.

"Thanks," he said, "but I can't come in."

"I didn't invite you in!"

"Good thing, because I have to work."

She compressed her pretty lips into a line. A memory of how they felt against his skin started to surface, but he deliberately shoved it back down.

Friendly thoughts.

"What do you want, Riley?"

He forced himself not to read any sexual meaning into her question. *Friendly.*

"Did you know that I like jazz enough to drive a hundred miles to hear a good band?"

"I didn't know that."

"I didn't think so. You and I don't really know much about each other at all. I don't even know if you like jazz."

Her eyes narrowed, as though she couldn't fathom what he was getting at. "As a matter of fact, I do," she said, but the admission sounded reluctant.

"Who do you prefer? Benny Goodman or Duke Ellington?"

"The Duke."

"Ella Fitzgerald, Billie Holiday or Sarah Vaughan?"

"Gotta go with Ella."

"Louis Armstrong or—"

"Stop right there," she interrupted.

"Because there isn't anybody better than Satchmo?"

She nodded and returned his smile. How could he have dated her for nearly a month and not known she shared his passion for jazz?

"So what do you say to driving to Savannah tonight?" he asked, pressing what finally felt like an advantage. "Razzamajazz isn't on the same level as the jazz greats, but the band is worth the drive."

"Go to Savannah? With you?" The smile was gone, the wariness back in her eyes.

"With me and my friends Lauren, Ben and Mark," he clarified. "You probably met them last year."

She shook her head. "I don't think so. You didn't introduce me to any of your friends last year."

That was yet another error he'd made the first

time around. He'd been so blinded by lust that he hadn't done the usual things that strengthened a couple's bond.

"I'll introduce you tonight," he offered. "We plan to have dinner on River Street, listen to the band and come back after their sets. I'm driving, so be ready at about six."

"I didn't say I'd go."

"You didn't say you wouldn't."

She pressed her lips together and he waited. Was this how a defendant felt before the jury came in with a verdict?

"I can't."

"Why not?" he asked, then watched her struggle to come up with an excuse.

"I'm going to Columbia today to check out some new furniture stores and to Christmas shop," she finally said. "I won't be back by six."

"Go to Columbia tomorrow."

She hesitated. "That's not possible."

His inclination was to press her to cancel her plans, partly because he suspected she'd invented them on the spur of the moment, but mostly because he wanted to spend the evening with her.

He forced himself to resist the urge.

"Maybe another time then," he said. "A group of us go out to listen to jazz a couple times a month."

He made the statement as though he considered her in the same category as his friends Ben and Mark.

Yeah, right, he thought with a burst of honesty a minute later, as he descended the stairs to the first floor.

Friendly thoughts be damned.

He never daydreamed about what Ben or Mark—or Lauren, for that matter—looked like naked under their clothes.

He consoled himself with the very small concession that at least his thoughts about Kate hadn't been *unfriendly*.

KATE REACHED FOR THE handrail as she climbed the stairs to the third floor, only to crush a section of artificial garland. Absently rubbing her palm, she noticed that the garland extended the entire length of the rail, with bright red bows positioned at every peak.

It was beginning to look a lot like Christmas everywhere she went.

Kate shook her head to rid it of the lyrics to the lively holiday song, but the strategy didn't work.

She hated to be a scrooge, but the truth was that the Christmas season reminded her of Riley. She'd tried to avoid him by going to Columbia this weekend, but had thought of him whenever she'd seen a tree, light or Santa Claus display.

Considering she'd spent most of her time in shopping malls, that had been constantly.

By getting a hotel room instead of making the two-hour drive back to Charleston, she'd made sure he wouldn't come knocking on her door last night.

And she'd successfully escaped him today, too. She'd lingered in her apartment only long enough to put away her packages and check her answering machine—two "I just called to chat" messages from Mom, none from Riley—before fleeing.

No, not fleeing. Leaving. She and Julia Carmichael, the newlywed who'd moved into the apartment above hers a month before, were having a girls' night.

"I'm so glad we're doing this," Julia told Kate a few minutes later while carrying a bowl of popcorn and a stack of DVDs into the TV room. "I hope you don't mind that I waited until Phil was on a sales trip to ask you over."

"I hear you," Kate said. "I know how busy a new husband can keep you."

"You can hear us?" Julia covered her mouth with the long, slender fingers of her right hand. "With your apartment below ours, I should have known. The bed creaks something awful, but maybe I can get Phil not to be so noisy."

Kate bit her bottom lip to stop the laughter from escaping, gathered her composure and said, "Julia, honey, I meant I heard what you were saying. Not that I could hear you and Phil."

"Oh." Julia was a natural blonde, with fair skin that could turn remarkably red. She looked so adorably embarrassed that Kate couldn't hold back a burst of laughter. Julia joined in after a moment, with inelegant guffaws that made Kate like her even better.

"You must think I'm terribly unsophisticated," Julia said when they'd stopped laughing.

"Terribly lucky, you mean. If Phil has a brother, you've got to introduce me."

"No brother," said Julia, wiping tears from under her eyes.

"How about a cousin? Friend? Co-worker? Male acquaintance?"

Julia's blue eyes widened. "You're serious? You want to be set up?"

"The sooner, the better."

"But haven't I seen you with, like, four different guys in the past few weeks?"

"Five," Kate corrected.

"If you can get five dates with five guys, what do you need me for?"

"I'm afraid I've exhausted the supply of eligible men I know personally."

Julia laughed. "Most of the teachers who work with me are female, but I'll ask Phil if he knows anybody. I think some single guys work in his office. Are you looking for anything in particular?"

"Yep." Kate clicked off the points on her fingers. "Male. Single. Straight."

"Ah, the trifecta. I'd suggest the guy downstairs if I didn't already know you two were just friends."

Friends. There was that word again. But maybe Julia wasn't referring to Riley. More than one man lived downstairs.

"Do you mean Thomas or Frederick?" she asked.

Julia scrunched up her pretty face. "You said you wanted the trifecta. Those two are the daily double. I was talking about Riley."

Kate groaned. "But Riley and I—"

The doorbell interrupted her half formed protest,

and Julia got to her feet. "Speaking of Riley, that's probably him now. He said he'd bring the pizza and beer."

Kate's heart bounced in her chest like a pinball. "You invited Riley?"

Julia maneuvered around the sofa. "He sort of invited himself. With you two being such good friends, I knew you wouldn't mind."

Kate didn't have enough time to brace herself before Riley strolled into the room wearing a faded denim shirt, a worn pair of jeans and a five o'clock shadow. How could a man built to wear a suit look even more delicious in old clothes?

"Hey, Kate." He slanted her a charming smile before setting down a six-pack of Dixie Beer and an aromatic box of hot pizza on the coffee table.

He headed directly for her, and she felt the urge to fan herself. How could he possibly think they could be friends? Hadn't he paid attention the other night? Hadn't he felt the heat then? Didn't he feel it now?

When he was inches away, he bent at the waist. What was he doing? She plastered herself against the back of the sofa cushion, but his clean, male scent still went to her head and made her feel dizzy. His face came close, closer, until it blurred out of focus. Then he kissed her…on the cheek.

Her skin tingled, heat swirled in her stomach and she felt like she might hyperventilate. He didn't seem to notice. He plopped down next to her. "Did I miss anything?"

"Not much." Julia trailed him into the room carrying paper plates and napkins. She put them down before taking a seat in an armchair at a right angle from the sofa. "Kate was asking if I knew anybody I could set her up with."

"Really?" Riley shot Kate an interested look. "I thought our Kate was already dating heavily."

"She is, but none of those guys do it for her. Right, Kate?"

"I wouldn't say that," Kate began.

"You just did, right before Riley got here," Julia said. "Hey, have you asked Riley if he knows anybody?"

Kate tried not to visibly recoil while she composed herself. "That would be a little weird considering Riley and I used to go out."

"You did? Good for you for managing to still be friends. But it doesn't solve your man-shortage problem," Julia said, then clapped. "Wait. I do know somebody. There's a really cute doctor in my Web site design class. He's nice, too."

"A doctor," Kate repeated, trying to sound impressed. "How do I meet him?"

"Five or six of us have started going out for drinks after class. Monday nights. Nine o'clock at Hanrahan's. I'm pretty sure he'll be there tomorrow."

"Then I'm there, too," Kate said.

"You could come, too, Riley," Julia offered. "For support."

"That's not such a good idea." Kate rushed to interject before Riley could reply. "I'm sure Riley has better things to do than helping me get a man."

"Whatever," Julia said as she flipped through the stack of DVDs. "Phil and I merged our collections. So what do you want to see? *While You Were Sleeping? When a Man Loves a Woman? Casablanca? The Last of the Mohicans?*"

"That last one," Kate said before Julia read off any more titles of romantic films. With Riley present, it was safer to stick to mayhem. "Seems to me I heard that one was good."

"It is," Julia agreed readily. "What do you think, Riley?"

"Pop it in," he said, stretching his arm over the back of the sofa.

Kate inched closer to the armrest, as far away from Riley as she could get, then fidgeted for the next two hours as Daniel Day-Lewis risked his life to protect Madeleine Stowe from the attacking Indians. "Stay alive," Daniel of the flowing mane and burgeoning pecs told Madeleine, "and I will find you."

"Isn't that the most romantic thing you've ever heard?" Julia asked on a sigh. "He found her, just like he said he would."

"What did it take him?" Riley asked as he munched on popcorn. "About five minutes of screen time? Kind of lessens the magnitude, don't you think?"

Kate didn't think so, but kept her opinion to herself. She voted to watch *The Terminator* next. She'd never seen it before, but had heard about its double-digit body count.

Nobody had ever told her that it was also a love story.

She wiped away tears from under her eyes as the credits scrolled up the television screen in a relentless climb when the movie ended. The theme music, with its compelling mechanical drumbeat, echoed inside her.

"Didn't you envy Linda Hamilton?" Julia remarked, sounding equally touched.

Kate sniffed. "Imagine having somebody love you so much they'd travel through time to save you."

"Envy her?" Riley snorted. "She spent the entire movie running for her life from an indestructible killer cyborg."

Kate merely looked at him and shook her head, angry at herself for the onslaught of wanting that had overtaken her as she'd sat next to him and watched the movies.

She'd wanted him eleven months ago and she wanted him still, the way Cora had wanted Hawkeye, the way the champion from the future had wanted Sarah. But she was wiser now. She knew he'd never fight Indians or travel through time for her.

"If you don't get it, it would take too long to explain." She unfolded her legs from under her and stood up. "And I've got to be going."

"You can't go," Julia protested. "It's only ten o'clock, and we still haven't watched *Braveheart*."

Kate shook her head. She wouldn't be suckered into watching another romance passing itself off as an action movie. She'd seen *Braveheart*. The main reason Mel Gibson donned blue face paint and led the bloody rebellion to free Scotland was because the English murdered his beloved wife.

"This is the longest I've sat still in years," she said, then added another excuse for good measure. "And my stomach's protesting from too much pizza and popcorn."

"Then let me walk you downstairs." Riley got to his feet.

"No, no." Dismayed at the shrillness she heard in her voice, Kate deliberately toned it down. "You stay here with Julia and Mel."

"No way," Riley said. "I'm pretty sure I've got something at my apartment for indigestion. What kind of friend would I be if I let you suffer?"

RILEY TRIED NOT TO LET the speed at which Kate descended the stairs to her apartment discourage him. She wanted to be rid of him, but he didn't have to make it easy for her.

"You should have come to the jazz club last night," he said when they were in the hallway. "Razzamajazz did a tribute to Satchmo, played all his music."

She whirled, her eyes rounded. "You're kidding!"

"Actually, I am kidding. I wanted you to feel bad for not going. Especially since they really did put on a good show."

"I told you," she said, "I had to Christmas shop."

"You also told me you have indigestion after eating one piece of pizza," he remarked as they approached their adjacent doors.

She kept her eyes averted as she fished her apartment key out of her jeans pocket. "It must have been the popcorn, then."

"How much popcorn did you have? Two handfuls or three?"

Kate threw up her hands. "Okay. You got me. I don't have indigestion. I said I did so I could leave."

"I thought you liked Julia."

"I do like Julia. It's you I have a problem with."

"What kind of a problem?"

"The friends thing," she blurted out, fire in her eyes. "I told you Friday night it wouldn't work. After tonight, I'm even more sure of it."

He wasn't. Yeah, he'd needed to strategically position a pillow on his lap at certain times during the night. But he'd acted like a friend, and intended to keep on acting that way. He'd listen to whatever she had to say, the way he hadn't listened last year.

"Tell me why you think a friendship between us won't work."

"You know why," she snapped. "Because we have a history."

"You mean our sexual history?"

Her eyes flashed. "Yes."

"I've been thinking about that," he said, which was the understatement of the millennium. "If we ignore it, it seems to me that maybe we can get past it."

"Ignore it!" She placed her soft, warm hand over his heart. It sped up at her touch. A pulse beat wildly in her throat. "How do you propose to ignore that?"

"Willpower?" he suggested.

She tilted her face up to his. All he'd need to do to claim her mouth was move fractionally forward.

"Do you really think we have enough of it?" she asked.

He breathed in the scent of her spicy perfume and felt his heart race at an even faster clip. He touched his forehead to hers, a trick he'd once used to try to slow down the ferocity with which he wanted her. It hadn't worked then. It didn't work now.

Her breath mingled with his and the familiar heat overtook him, as though he were standing next to a raging furnace. His control shattered. Cradling the back of her head, he dragged her mouth to his.

The instant their lips met, a thick ribbon of heat blasted through him. She tasted faintly of popcorn, but he could stop eating popcorn after a few handfuls. He'd never get enough of Kate and this powerful passion that sprouted whenever he touched her. He anchored a hand at her back, gathering her closer against him.

He'd kissed a number of women in an attempt to forget her, to forget *this,* but none of them compared to Kate. With one of his hands tangled in her hair, he dipped to taste her again and again.

Why had he let her go? Why hadn't he fought harder to hold on to what he couldn't live without?

She opened her mouth in invitation, and he deepened the kiss as her hands explored the muscular breadth of his shoulders. His tongue tangled with hers, and familiar sensations tore through him with sensual power.

This explosion of need was nothing new. It had ignited every time they'd kissed this way.

With a ferocity that made beads of sweat break out on his forehead, he wanted to tear off her clothes, lower her to the floor and drive into her until they were both mindless with pleasure.

A year ago, he would have done exactly that.

However, surrendering to his impulses had yielded great sex but little else. It hadn't built a bond strong enough to keep them together. Sex wouldn't be enough now, either, not until they gave themselves time to get to know each other out of bed.

Going against every impulse he possessed, he lifted his head and broke off the kiss.

He strived to appear calm and controlled while fighting the nearly overwhelming temptation to drag her mouth back to his.

She took a shuddering breath. When he swept the hair from her eyes, his hands trembled with the effort of restraining himself.

But he couldn't abandon the plan. This was too important. *She* was too important. He swallowed, managing to make his voice sound normal when he said, "I still think we should get to know one another better before we sleep together."

She batted his hand away. "I'm not going to sleep with you! I only let you kiss me to prove a point."

Her lips were swollen, her eyes still hazy with desire. He clamped his mouth shut before theorizing that she wanted him more than she wanted to be right.

He dropped hands that still itched to reach for her, stepped back and affected a shrug.

"That's probably the right call," he said after he'd covered the few steps to his apartment. Before he went inside, he looked directly at her and carefully kept his voice light. "We need to give this friends thing more time."

4

KATE ENTERED HANRAHAN'S the following night determined to stop fuming over the ridiculous spin Riley had put on that searing kiss they'd shared.

He'd somehow twisted things to make it seem as though he wanted friendship while she was angling for sex.

Been there, done that, regretted it.

She could find someone else to have sex with, thank you very much. Someone who might actually want more than sex from her. Maybe it would even be the cute doctor she was coming here to meet.

An assortment of beer drinkers sat at the bar watching overhead televisions broadcasting a college basketball game, but the real action came from the three musicians performing on a back stage.

Kate spotted Julia waving to her from a large, rectangular rear table not far from the pulsating music.

She straightened the hip-hugging jersey-knit miniskirt she wore with high, black boots and black tights, rubbed her lips together to evenly distribute her recently applied gloss and walked determinedly toward the table.

The table was long and narrow, with seats on either side that were filled with six of Julia's friends.

Kate's determination rose. If she were so hot for Riley, she wouldn't be taking Julia up on her offer to introduce her to a new man. Now would she?

She scanned the table for the cute guy Julia had told her about, but her gaze snagged on the face she'd stroked and the hair she'd run her fingers through barely twenty-four hours ago. Riley. He lifted a hand in greeting.

Her ire rose. Trust Riley to show up now to ruin things when he'd made himself scarce since the kiss. He probably...

The theory short-circuited when Riley turned away from her and toward the woman next to him. She had a gamine face, jet-black hair cut to fit her head like a cap and a killer smile.

Who was she, and what was Riley doing here with her?

"Kate, over here," Julia called, indicating an empty seat next to her and across the table from Riley.

Kate pasted on a smile that hurt the corners of her mouth to maintain, marched over to the empty seat, smoothed her skirt and sat down.

"Everybody, this is my friend Kate," Julia said loudly to be heard above the lead singer, who strummed an electric guitar as he performed a song that sounded like a cross between reggae and rap.

Kate nodded at each person in turn as Julia introduced them, making very sure she didn't alter her expression when they got to Riley. Even when he winked at her.

When the introductions were behind them, the only name Kate could remember belonged to the woman making moon eyes at Riley.

Lana Murphy.

On closer inspection, she seemed to be about ten years older than Riley. Kate examined her for flaws and found one in a slight overbite, but the imperfection made her more attractive.

"I love your outfit," Lana told her in a loud, friendly voice. "The fishnet sleeves on your sweater are to die for."

"Thank you," Kate said, but Lana had already turned that beaming smile back on Riley. Possibly because carrying a conversation over the table was impossible, but Kate didn't think so.

Kate elbowed Julia and spoke directly into her ear to be heard over the music. "What's Riley doing here?"

"I ran into him this morning and mentioned he should come," Julia said, then nodded across the table to where Riley and Lana sat huddled together. "He seems to be having a good time, don't you think?"

"Actually, I—"

"So what do you think of Matt? He's cute, isn't he?" Julia interrupted before Kate could say she doubted Lana was Riley's type.

"Matt who?"

Julia rolled her eyes. "The doctor. He's sitting right next to you. So talk to him already."

Kate turned, and there was a cute doctor, just like Julia said. He was maybe five years older than her, with the kind of all-American good looks that made Kate think of apple pie and lemonade. He had dimples and sky-blue eyes that roamed over her face in apparent appreciation.

"Hi. I'm Kate."

His dimples deepened. "I know who you are. I paid attention when Julia introduced you. What are you drinking?"

"A gin and tonic."

He signaled a waitress—no small feat considering the size of the bar crowd. Somehow he conveyed her choice of drink over the music. A gin and tonic sat in front of her in less than a minute.

"Thank you," she said, and asked Matt about himself. She listened as he told her about the rewards of pediatrics, coaching his nephew's T-ball team and the pro bono work he did for a homeless shelter.

Across the table, Lana had inched her chair closer to Riley's. Was Riley interested in Lana? Kate couldn't tell. He didn't shy away from the other woman, but didn't lean toward her, either.

"I'm taking Web design as a lark because it's totally different than medicine," Matt was saying. "So now everybody at work calls me Dr. Geek."

Focus on the cute doctor, Kate told herself. *Say something. Anything.*

"I'm sure you make a great geek," she said.

He laughed. "Enough about me. Let's hear about

you. Julia says you're an interior designer. Are you in business for yourself or do you work for a firm?"

She told him about Designs on You, explaining, when he asked, that she hoped to move from residential to hospitality design. "I'm only twenty-six so I haven't tackled any truly big projects yet, but I'm building a portfolio that…"

Lana let loose with a trill of laughter, and Kate's voice trailed off into silence. Laying a hand on Riley's arm, Lana continued to talk into his ear. Riley stared straight ahead, his eyes locked on Kate's.

She'd told him while they were dating that he looked best in shades of red. He wore the color tonight, which could explain his high hunk quotient. But then, he looked even better without any clothes at all.

Her body heated, the sensation not unlike the one she got from the warm rush of water in the shower. Annoyed with herself, she broke eye contact and turned back to Matt.

"What's going on?" he asked softly, not that anyone else could hear them with the band blaring. "Who is that guy across the table to you?"

"I don't know what you mean," she lied.

"Sure you do. You can't help looking at him. Is he somebody you used to go out with, or somebody you want to go out with?"

"Used to," Kate reluctantly admitted. "But it's been over for almost a year. There's nothing between us now."

"Really?" One of his eyebrows rose.

"Really." She snuck another glance at Riley and met the brown of his eyes before quickly looking away. "I think he's trying to make time with Lana. What's her story anyway?"

"A single mom. Divorced about ten years. Works in North Charleston cutting hair. She's taking the class to earn extra money so she can design and maintain a Web site for the beauty shop," Matt answered, then gave her a penetrating look.

"I only asked because Riley and I are friends."

"Really?" That single eyebrow arched again. His eyes were clear and interested, inspiring confidences.

"No, not really," Kate admitted. "Friendship is what Riley says he wants, but I'm pretty sure he wants to sleep with me."

"Then he's still in love with you?"

The lead singer leaped around the stage like he was auditioning to be the next headliner for the Rolling Stones, belting out what barely passed for a tune. Kate leaned closer to Matt to make sure what she said was private.

"That's the thing. He's never been in love with me. A man doesn't have to be in love with a woman to want sex from her, you know."

"I know," Matt said.

The Rolling Stone wannabe announced the band was taking a break. The bar seemed unnaturally quiet for a few seconds before the jukebox kicked in, but Kate still couldn't pick up any of Lana and Riley's conversation.

Julia tugged on her sleeve, then leaned close to whisper in her ear. "What do you think of Matt?"

"He's a very nice man," Kate answered truthfully.

"Then ask him out," Julia ordered before she went back to talking to the heavyset man on her other side.

Why not? Not only was Matt a nice man, but he was a good listener. Kate could do far worse. *Here goes*, she thought.

"I've had a good time talking to you tonight, Matt," she said. "Would you like to go out sometime?"

"Yes," Matt said, "but I have a policy against dating women who are still hung up on their ex-boyfriends."

"I'm not—"

"You are." Matt's smile looked sad. "If that ever changes, give me a call. Julia knows where I work."

"You're wrong," Kate said, watching the way the strong column of Riley's throat constricted as he took a swallow of beer. He raised his mug to her and she quickly looked away.

"I'd love to be wrong," he said, "but I don't think so."

Kate spent the next fifteen minutes avoiding eye contact with Riley to prove her point, but the effort exhausted her. When the band once again took the stage, she nudged Julia's elbow. "I'm taking off."

Julia's eyebrows twinkled. "With Matt?"

"That didn't work out, but thanks for thinking of me," she said, then rose before Julia could quiz her.

She mouthed goodbye to the people at the table, careful not to single Riley out for special attention.

With a little wave, she moved quickly away from the table toward the exit and tried not to think about when Riley would leave the bar. Or who would be with him when he did.

She emerged into the night, took her car keys from her purse, hit the button that automatically unlocked the driver's side door and jumped at the feel of a hand on her shoulder.

She whirled, only to come face-to-face with Riley. He removed his hand, but her heart rate didn't decrease.

"Sorry. I didn't mean to scare you. I called for you to wait up, but you must not have heard."

"It was hard to hear anything in there," she said, although the same wasn't true of the parking lot. The acoustics, if anything, seemed too clear. But then, the night seemed especially bright, too.

"I said I'd walk you to your car," he explained.

When she realized she was watching his lips, she raised her eyes to his. They weren't blue like Matt's, but the color of coffee with a dash of cream. So why did she, who liked her colors vivid, prefer brown to blue?

"You didn't have to do that," she said. "You don't want Lana to think we have something going on."

"You and I do have something going on."

Shivers danced up her spine, but she tried to sound forbidding. "You're not going to try to kiss me again, are you?" she asked, even as she realized that half of her—not including the half containing her brain—hoped he would.

He laughed, and his teeth showed white against the darkness of the sky. "No, I'm not going to kiss you. When I said we had something going on, I meant a friendship."

"Oh," she said, telling herself she was not disappointed.

"How about you and Matt? Was that a friendship I saw developing, or something more?"

The headlights of a car searching for a parking place caught them in its beam, and she figured their parking lot chat had gone on long enough.

She closed the distance between herself and her car, with Riley trailing her. "I don't want to talk to you about Matt."

"Why not? I thought we agreed to give this friends thing more time."

"I didn't agree to that."

She turned to address him when she reached her car. He moved forward, not touching her but effectively trapping her between his body and the car.

She saw his eyes dip to her mouth. His head bowed, until only inches separated their lips and she could feel his whisper-soft breath. If he kissed her, she wouldn't do anything to stop him.

"I really want to be your friend, Kate," he murmured, then, inexplicably, he straightened.

She felt instantly bereft, then angry at herself because of it. She swung open the car door and scrambled to get inside.

"No," she said before she was entirely settled.

He put a hand on her car door, preventing her from closing it. "No what?"

No, I can't be your friend, she thought. But she'd already told him that. She didn't see any point in repeating it.

"No, Matt and I are not starting anything," she said instead, then rolled her eyes. She was at a loss to understand why she'd confided in him, especially when she'd had an excellent chance to convince him she was interested in somebody else.

Don't ask, she told herself, but couldn't resist. Not when he seemed to be in a confiding kind of mood. "How about you and Lana?"

He seemed surprised. "She's nice, but I'm not interested in Lana that way."

"Why not?"

"She's not my type." His eyes ran over her with naked appreciation, working upward until he focused on her lips. A cool breeze swept across the parking lot and blew into the car, but she felt overheated.

She didn't waste any time in shutting the car door when he removed his hand. If he guessed her body temperature had spiked to unnatural levels, who knew what he might infer? He might even claim that she wanted to take him home to bed.

She told herself not to glance into the rearview mirror as she drove off, but her eyes strayed anyway.

Riley stood in the middle of the parking lot, watching her go. He cut a tall, impressive figure, with his hands shoved in the pockets of his brown leather jacket and the wind whipping through the short strands of his hair.

The warmth that had invaded her body grew more pronounced, and she could no longer lie to herself.

He was right. A part of her wanted to resume their sexual relationship, but she wasn't stupid enough or weak enough to give in to it.

She'd traveled this road before and knew it could only end in heartache.

TWELVE-HOUR WORKDAYS didn't leave much time left over for building a friendship, Riley thought as he popped the tab on a beer can and took a pull.

Especially when the potential friend was avoiding him.

He sat down at the table for two in his subletted apartment's tiny kitchen and propped his stocking feet on an empty chair.

He was doing the right thing by taking things slowly. Friends didn't crowd each other. They didn't let themselves get so frustrated at not having seen her since last night that they pounced as soon as she came into the building.

Better to wait for opportunity to strike, so it would look like he'd run into her accidentally.

His apartment faced the street, and at the sound of a car engine, he rose and looked out his bay window to see Kate's electric-green Toyota pull up to the curb.

He headed for his front door, thinking it fortuitous that he'd forgotten to check his mail slot on the way in. Never mind that he'd yet to visit the post office and have his mail forwarded from Sullivan's Island.

He reached the foyer a few seconds before Kate came in from the cold. When she saw him, her dark eyes turned guarded. Tonight she wore a thigh-length red coat with a flared hem and high-heeled black boots that nearly reached her knees.

She'd had the same coat last year. He remembered one particular day when he'd been in such a hurry to make love to her that one of the buttons had popped in his haste to get her naked and under him.

Keep it light, he reminded himself. *Keep it friendly.*

"Hey, Kate," he said, going to the wall and feigning surprise at his empty mail slot. "Nothing for me today, I guess. I forgot to check the mail earlier. Still not used to the new place."

Was that too much information? Should he shut up now?

"Hey," she said, moving to her own mail slot.

Her shoulder passed within six inches of his, and he refrained from leaning toward her like a man intent on being more than her friend.

"You're home late," he remarked.

Not, *Where the hell have you been? Or, Who were you with?* Just a simple, friendly observation.

"I went out to dinner."

The Kate he'd known last year would have expanded on the statement, although, in retrospect, their conversations had been lacking. She hadn't talked much about herself, and he sure as hell hadn't opened a vocal chord and bled words of get-to-know-me-better wisdom.

"By yourself?" he prodded.

"I don't like to eat alone."

Although her dining companion could have been female, he got the impression she'd been with a man. Another date?

"You go out to dinner a lot," he remarked.

"I don't like to cook, so it's either dinner out or sandwiches in."

Her eyes met his, and he was aware of time ticking by.

"I've got an early meeting tomorrow morning," she finally said, "so I really should get upstairs."

"You work too hard," he said, moving slightly to let her by.

"You leave in the mornings before I do," she said on her way past.

"I've been putting in a lot of hours because of the hotel," he said, then tried a last-ditch attempt to stop her from dashing up the stairs. "Hey, you should drop by, see how it's going."

To his surprise, she stopped and turned. Interest lit her eyes. "Do you mean it?"

"Sure, I'll even give you a tour," he said, surprised that it had worked. "I'll be at the site most of the morning tomorrow. Come by anytime."

"Thanks. I've been curious about the hotel since you started building it, so I just might do that," she said with a ghost of a smile. Inclining her head slightly, she practically ran up the stairs.

Patience, he reminded himself as he watched her go.

If he kept extending the branches of friendship, one of these days she just might grab hold.

THE HIGH HEELS OF KATE'S boots wobbled over the uneven ground as she approached the construction site. The landscaping, she knew, wouldn't come until the final phase of the project.

She shielded her eyes against the late-morning sun and tried to gauge the job's progress. The foundation had been poured, steel beams and columns had been erected and workers were in the process of putting up walls and windows.

Very soon a hotel would emerge from the raw ingredients.

She tilted her head, trying to envision the finished product. It would be stunning, she concluded. Riley had cleverly designed five separate wings that shot off from a central lobby. Her designer's eye pictured the space as airy and electric, decorated in rich hues and stunning accent pieces.

A tall man in jeans, work boots and a hard hat broke off from a cluster of workers and walked in her direction. His coloring and build were similar to Riley's, but he walked faster. He was also slightly taller and a good bit broader.

Not Riley, but his brother Dave.

"Hey, there. Can I help you?" he asked when he got within hearing range.

She was about to ask where she could find Riley when he pointed a finger at her. "Wait a minute. I know you. You used to go out with my brother. Kate, isn't it?"

She nodded. "Kate Marino. We met last December at that little Thai place on King Street."

She didn't add that Riley never would have introduced them if not for chance. Dave had been lunching alone, and she and Riley had happened into the restaurant.

"What are you doing here?" he asked abruptly.

"I'm here to see Riley. Is he around?"

"Does he know you're coming?"

Taken aback by his gruffness, she nodded. "He said he'd give me a tour."

"He's in the trailer, but I don't want you any closer to the site without a hard hat," he said after a long pause. "Wait here and I'll let Riley know where you are."

Without another word, he headed back toward the site, unclipping the cell phone from his belt and punching in a number as he walked. Talk about being dismissed, she thought.

She wrapped her arms around herself, even though today was unusually warm, and the red leather jacket she wore with low-waisted, flared black pants was protection enough against the weakened bite of the December wind.

Within moments, Riley emerged from the silver trailer at the edge of the site, carrying an extra hard hat. He wore one, too, but unlike his brother, he'd dressed in street clothes. Not his usual khakis and casual jacket, either, but dark pants and a black leather jacket. Her heart pounded a little faster.

She knew architects lined up their next jobs while working on their current ones and wondered if he was meeting with prospective clients later.

"I'm glad you came," he said when he reached her, touching her lightly on the arm.

"I'm not sure I am." She chewed on her lower lip. In the distance, his brother barked orders at a forklift operator. "I don't think Dave likes me."

"Don't take it personally. He's been so grouchy lately that the guys have been calling him Oscar."

"It's more than that." She transferred her gaze from the older brother to the younger. The usual jolt of attraction hit her but she was getting better at ignoring it. "I'm pretty sure it's because of some wrong he thinks I did you."

"He's being protective, is all. He knows how we ended."

She looked away, because rehashing the past wouldn't serve any useful purpose. But she got the idea that Riley hadn't told his brother the entire story.

"I'm impressed with your work," she said to change the subject. "I can see that the hotel's design will complement the architecture of the aquarium, which is amazing considering the aquarium's so modern and you went with traditional."

"You can see that?" He seemed pleased. "I don't think you can treat a building as a solitary object without regard for its setting. It has to derive meaning from its context, and here the context is a historic city with a contemporary aquarium."

"So you tried to please both worlds?"

"I went with the Federal style because you see the details in modern buildings all the time, like the arch of a Palladian window or the fanlight over the front door. I thought the Federalist lines suited the project, too. They're curved instead of square and angular." Riley's words spilled out so fast, they nearly ran together—a noted departure from his usual slow, measured speech. "Here, let me show you."

His eyes shining and his expression animated, he reached for her hand. His felt solid and warm and caused a tingle to run up her arm. What was it about men who loved what they did that made them so sexy?

"The hotel will be five stories with two hundred rooms and six thousand square feet of meeting space." He spoke loudly to be heard above the construction noise. "Charleston Place has twenty-two thousand, but the Hotel Charleston developers aren't overly interested in the business trade.

"See that, through there? That'll be the free-falling staircase which will lead to a grand ballroom. It'll be geometrically shaped, like all the other meeting rooms and open spaces."

"I can picture it," she said. "I'd go with a water theme, because you've got the aquarium on one side of the hotel and the Cooper River on the other. Cobalt decor with gold accents. Custom carpeting in a wave pattern, crystal raindrops on the chandeliers and those Palladium windows looking out over the river."

"Through there will be a courtyard, fountain and one of those small gardens Charleston is famous for. And over there's the entranceway." He pointed toward some beams and columns. "It'll open up into the lobby, which you can overlook from the second floor."

"Maybe with a gleaming wraparound reception desk and a grand chandelier with more of those crystal raindrops," she said, feeding off his excitement. "I can see sofas and chairs in shades of blue, and a green atrium."

He grinned at her. "It sounds like you've given this some thought."

"Every designer in town has, at one time or other," she said. "I'd have encouraged Designs on You to put in a bid for the interiors if that investment group that hired you hadn't already contracted with another firm."

"I didn't know you were interested in commercial design."

"My interest is evolving," she confided. "I've mostly done residential projects, but I worked on a hotel renovation earlier this year and I've been itching to do more hospitality work."

"Why don't you specialize then?"

"Commercial design jobs don't hang on trees. It takes time to carve out a reputation and get to the point where people will trust you. But, of course, you know that."

"I know it's important in all situations to build trust."

He met her eyes and she knew he was no longer talking about hotel construction and design. He still held her hand, which suddenly seemed awkward. She started to pull it away, but he tightened his grip.

"Kate, I—"

"Hey, Riley. I need some advice over here," Dave shouted from twenty feet away.

While he was momentarily distracted, Kate pulled her hand the rest of the way from his and backed up. She didn't want to hear what he had to say, didn't want it to make a difference.

"I've got to go anyway," she said. "I've taken up enough of your time."

"Look, it's nearly lunchtime." He no longer had hold of her hand but managed to keep her in place with his eyes. "Let me see what my brother wants and then we can grab a bite."

A powerful desire to accept his offer rose in Kate, frightening her. What was happening here?

"I can't." She shook her head. "I've got to go."

When she'd gotten only a few steps away, he stopped her with a word. "Kate?"

She turned only her head.

"I'm really glad you came."

She nodded, then walked quickly to her car, aware of his eyes on her back, her emotions in turmoil.

She wasn't glad she'd come. She wasn't glad at all.

5

ENCOURAGED BY KATE'S visit to the job site, Riley took the steps to his second-floor apartment two by two. Operation I-want-to-be-friends was finally paying dividends.

His strategy was to ratchet up the charm, striking when her defenses were down. He would offer to feed her the beef stew that had been simmering in his Crock-Pot all day. He didn't often take the time to cook, but this morning he'd thrown the stew together with an eye toward sharing it.

Her car, for once, was out front, meaning she was home.

A shadow covered the opening at the top of the stairs. He stopped abruptly, barely in time to avoid plowing into Julia Carmichael.

"And here I thought you Charleston boys took things slowly." Julia settled her hands on her hips. "I guess that doesn't include the stairs."

"Sorry," Riley said sheepishly. "I guess I was in a hurry to get home."

"Hmm, that's interesting, considering you live alone."

"Why's that?" he asked, aiming for nonchalant.

"Because in my experience, most people are eager to get to a some*one* rather than a some*thing*," she said, then winked.

"Why do I get the feeling you think you know something?"

"Because I do," she said saucily. "I was at the bar Monday night."

"I appreciate you introducing us, Julia, but things with Lana and I aren't going anywhere."

"I'm not talking about Lana. I'm talking about Kate."

"I'm working on becoming Kate's friend," he said slowly.

Her eyebrows arched. "Oh, really? Well, that's an interesting way to put it."

She stepped aside to let him pass. He didn't realize she'd followed him down the hall until her voice stopped him before he could knock on Kate's door. "She's not home."

"Her car's out front," he pointed out.

"So is Andy's car."

"Who's Andy?"

"This pushy guy who works with my husband. Phil introduced him to Kate tonight."

"Why'd you let your husband introduce Kate to a pushy guy?" he asked, hearing the exasperation in his voice.

"I didn't know he was pushy. How could I when I didn't meet him until tonight, either?"

"So where are they if they're not here?"

"They went for a walk to the Battery. Andy suggested drinks but Kate nixed that idea. Maybe she noticed he was pushy, too."

"Thanks," he said.

"Don't mention it," she tossed over her shoulder while walking away. "I'm always glad to help friendship along."

He dismissed her cryptic comment and went inside his apartment. Ignoring the fragrant smell of beef stew, he stripped off his shirt as he headed for his bedroom.

Work had kept him so busy that it had been days since he'd gotten in a run. With the temperature hovering around fifty, tonight boasted the perfect weather for a workout.

The best place on the peninsula for a short run was a loop around the Historic District that included the wide strip of sidewalk along the sea wall that bordered the Charleston harbor and led to the Battery.

And if he happened to accidentally run into Kate and this Andy character, so much the better.

Julia had said Andy was pushy. It wouldn't hurt to make sure he didn't try to push Kate somewhere she didn't want to go.

Ten minutes later, Riley kept his pace constant and his breathing even as he ran alongside the blue-black water of the harbor.

He usually admired the beauty of the grand, old houses aligning wide, quiet Murray Boulevard, but tonight his eyes pointed straight ahead.

It felt colder beside the water because of the breeze, but he found it refreshing. He'd spent most of the day cooped up in his office, working on ideas for a restaurant for which the Lowcountry Group had asked him to submit plans.

He squinted, picking out two figures in the distance roughly on line with the cannons pointing to Fort Sumter.

The figures grew in proportion as he got closer. A woman and a man. He increased his pace. The woman had short, sassy dark hair and wore a red leather jacket. Kate. The man, slightly taller with a slim build and a crew cut, looked like a chump. Andy.

They seemed to be discussing something. Kate's posture was vintage touch-me-not—stiff shoulders, arms crossed over her chest, a torso angled slightly away from the man.

As Riley's strides took him relentlessly nearer, the man—Andy the chump—grasped her by the shoulders and pulled her toward him.

"Hey, get your hands off her," Riley yelled.

The wind must have carried his voice because both their heads swiveled in his direction. He quickly closed the remaining distance until he was within a few steps of them.

He registered shock on Kate's face but was more concerned with the pair of male hands that still held her by the shoulders.

"Who the hell are you?" the chump bit out.

"A friend of Kate's who's telling you to let go of her."

The man dropped his hands but not his bravado. Kate stepped in front of him and sent an equally unfriendly glare Riley's way.

"Just what do you think you're doing, Riley Carter?"

Splotches of red appeared on her cheeks and temper sparked her eyes, causing him to question himself.

"Helping you?" he answered.

She settled her hands on her hips. "If I'd wanted your help, I would have asked for it."

"It seems to me that the person she needs help getting rid of is you," the chump said, sidestepping her.

Kate stepped sideways, too, positioning herself between the two of them. Riley got the feeling she was trying to protect him, which was ludicrous considering he had three or four inches and fifty pounds on the other man.

"Don't be ridiculous. I'm perfectly capable of ridding myself of men I can't trust." She directed the comment at the chump, but kept her eyes on Riley.

The mile he'd run from his Ashley Avenue sublet to the Battery hadn't stolen his breath, but her comment did.

"I want to go back now, Andy," she said, still watching Riley. "The walk's lost its appeal."

When the chump looked like he was about to take her arm, Riley found his voice. "I'll walk her back."

"No, you won't," Kate said before the chump could respond. "I came here with Andy. I'll go back with him."

"But—"

"The best thing you could do is run along." She shouldered past him before walking away with the chump, who looked back over his shoulder to glare at Riley.

Riley debated making another stab at convincing Kate she'd be safer walking home with him, but then she effortlessly knocked away the arm Andy tried to put around her.

Despite the mess he'd made of things, Riley smiled.

Kate was right. She could take care of herself.

KATE WATCHED THE TAILLIGHTS of Handy Andy's car get smaller as he drove north on Ashley Avenue and, thereby, out of her life.

She'd mentally started to refer to him by the nickname partway through their walk, when he talked about working with clay sculptures while trying to cop a feel.

She supposed he'd been trying to get across the message that he was good with his hands.

Maybe she shouldn't have been angry at Riley for happening along. She could have handled Andy by herself, but Riley's chance appearance had set her rejection in motion.

The little Honda that Julia drove pulled up to the curb, and she waited for her friend to get out of the car. Julia carried a bag from a nearby drugstore, which she swung in time with her steps.

"I suppose this means things didn't work out with Andy?" Julia said when she reached her.

"You don't seem surprised."

"I'm not. But suppose you tell me what happened anyway?"

"He was a little too, shall we say, *hands on* for my taste."

Julia hooked an elbow through hers and steered her toward the house. "I'll take my husband to task for recommending him, but isn't he the kind of guy you said you wanted?"

"I don't think so. He tried to talk me into sleeping with him fifteen minutes after we met."

"There you go." Laughter spiked Julia's voice. "You said you were looking for somebody who was crazy about you. Andy obviously was."

"I want somebody crazily in love with me, not crazily in lust."

"Same thing."

"They're not the same thing at all. You don't have to like a person to lust after them." Kate thought that over. "Well, *I'd* have to. But men usually aren't so discriminating."

"Riley seems to like you," Julia said, "and I'd say he's definitely lusting, too."

Kate stopped walking, which brought Julia to a jarring halt. "Why would you say that?"

"Oh, let's see." Julia put a finger to her chin, obviously only feigning thoughtfulness. "I know. The fact that you two were making eyes at each other at Hanrahan's."

"We were not!"

"Matt says you were. Remember the cute doctor

you mysteriously didn't hit it off with? He said it was because there's still something between you and Riley."

"Matt is imagining things."

"Then why did Riley ask me those twenty questions about you and Andy when I ran into him earlier on the staircase?"

Kate's mind reeled as her chance encounter with Riley no longer seemed so random. "Did you tell Riley that Andy and I were down at the Battery?"

"I mentioned it. Why?" Julia came up with the answer before Kate could reply. "He went down there, didn't he?"

"He sure did." Kate shook her head. "I knew that friendship stuff he's been spouting was a crock."

"He seemed sincere enough to me about wanting to be your friend."

"What he really wants is to be my lover," Kate said, fuming.

"Let's see. Gorgeous guy who turns you on. I need some enlightenment here, because I'm not understanding why this is a problem."

"Because the sex between us is great, that's why!"

"Still not understanding."

"Don't you see, Julia? We already broke up once because the only thing that worked between us was the sex. Now we're living next door to each other. Of course he's remembering how good things were in bed."

"I'm sure there's a convoluted logic to all this, but I'm not seeing it."

"It's a ploy. He doesn't want to be my friend. He wants to sleep with me."

"Because he likes you."

"No." Julia shook her head. "Because I'm convenient."

"*And* because he likes you."

"Maybe he does like me. But if I'd mattered to him, the way the person you're sleeping with is supposed to matter, he would have shown up to make things right way before now."

"I'm not sure I buy that, but let me play devil's advocate," Julia said. "Let's say you're not the love of Riley's life. So what? What's wrong with indulging yourselves with great sex for as long as it lasts?"

"What's wrong is that we've already been there and done that. And it didn't work out. What's wrong is that he's lying to get what he really wants."

"Then what are you going to do about it?"

"I'm going to drive him crazy," Kate said decisively.

"Then you *are* going to sleep with him?"

"Heck, no," Kate said. "I'm going to call his bluff."

AFTER HE DRIED OFF from his shower, Riley pulled on soft, gray sweatpants and an old T-shirt, and finger-combed his damp hair. He usually felt invigorated after a run, but not tonight.

Tonight he felt like a screwup.

How could he have let his testosterone run rampant like that and rushed to the rescue, when Kate clearly didn't need rescuing? Why hadn't he learned from his reckless, ill-advised charge into last year's disastrous affair?

He was hardly ever rash. Rash didn't work for him.

The plan wasn't to act like a caveman. It was to convince Kate to be his friend.

Under the circumstances, asking her to share his beef stew seemed like a very bad idea. Hell, he'd be lucky if she ever talked to him again.

Resigned to eating a dinner for one, he dished himself a bowl of steaming hot stew and tore a hunk of French bread from the loaf.

The doorbell interrupted him before the first spoonful reached his mouth. He put down the utensil with a clatter. Could it be Kate? It took him mere seconds to reach the door, but less time than that to talk sense to himself.

If Kate had deemed to speak to him again, it wouldn't be about anything pleasant.

He checked the peephole and got a distorted view of her face. If she looked lovely to him with her features wildly out of proportion, he thought, he had it bad.

Composing himself, he pulled opened the door and waited for her to blast him.

"Can I come in?" she asked instead.

Nothing in her expression hinted at anger boiling below the surface. Her mouth curved in a slight smile, and her dark eyes looked bright and innocent.

"Sure." He stepped aside to give her room. There

should have been ample space to get by, but her soft, full breast brushed his arm as she passed.

He felt as though he'd been scorched, but didn't react to the contact. She moved into the apartment in the easy way of someone who'd been there a hundred times, even kicking off her high heels and moving them off to the side.

"You don't mind, do you? I like to get comfortable when I'm not at work." She stretched her arms over her head and arched her back. His eyes zoomed to her breasts. The clingy material of her yellow top outlined their generous shape perfectly. She unfastened the top two buttons of her shirt, revealing cleavage. Sweat beaded on his brow. "There. That's better. Now I feel so much more relaxed."

Riley found his voice. "You came over here to relax?"

"I came over here because I smelled something delicious when I was in the hall. Stew, right?"

"Right."

"So what do you say? Can I bum dinner?"

"Sure," he said slowly, hardly able to believe his scenario of sharing his dinner was about to come true. "I was going to offer but thought you'd say no."

She turned innocent eyes to him. "Why's that?"

He scratched his head, absently noting his hair was still damp. Was this really happening? "I thought you were pissed at me for what happened down at the Battery."

"Oh, that. I was, but I'm over it." She waved it off

with a flick of her wrist, then went into the kitchen, leaving him no choice but to follow. Her sweet, rounded bottom moved provocatively as she walked. His gaze drifted lower, to her shapely legs, which were outlined by fishnet tights with a back seam subtly entwined with gold thread. He sucked in a breath.

"What are you waiting for?" She stood in his small kitchen, surrounded by banks of cabinets. "Aren't you going to dish me up a bowl of stew?"

Her question made him realize he'd stopped in his tracks. "Sure," he said, swallowing hard. He took his time opening a cabinet and removing a bowl, careful not to let his gaze stray to her exposed cleavage.

She stood next to the Crock-Pot, waiting on him. He expected her to move to give him room but she didn't budge. He got a whiff of wild-berry body lotion. She used to keep bottles of the stuff in her bathroom, and the scent immediately transported him back to the times they'd made love in the shower, when the spray had streamed over their naked bodies while they'd taken pleasure in each other.

He picked up the ladle and lifted the lid on the Crock-Pot, thankful that the smell of the stew overcame the scent of berries. Holding the ladle in his right hand and the bowl in his left, he poured the stew into the bowl.

She peered into the Crock-Pot and her left shoulder brushed his. It wasn't enough to jar him but his hand shook anyway, and some of the hot stew splashed on him.

"Quick, get that hand under some cold water," she said, taking the bowl from him and setting it down on the counter.

She switched the faucet on high, grabbed him by the wrist and thrust his hand under the water. The soothing cold streamed over his skin, but other parts of him still hissed. She stood so close that the entire left side of her body touched his. When he glanced down, he saw the valley between her breasts.

"I'm fine," he said after a moment, turning off the faucet and pulling his hand away. He took two quick steps back.

"Seems that was too hot for you to handle." Her eyes danced as they locked on his. Was she flirting with him? The breath snagged in his throat. "Tell you what. I'll carry the bowl to the table. You get the spoon and some of that yummy-looking French bread. It'll be safer that way."

She put the lid back on the Crock-Pot and picked up the bowl of stew, brushing by him again as she went to the table. That couldn't have been a coincidence, could it?

At the table, she sat down on one of the chairs, tucking her left leg under her. Her eyes seemed to glitter when she looked at him but it could have been a trick of the overhead light.

"I'm starved," she said, and he thought of sex instead of food. "I'd start eating, but my mother taught me to wait until everybody else at the table was ready. And you're not even sitting down."

She was right. He'd been so busy trying to read

her signals, and to figure out the cause of her recent about-face, that he'd yet to get the spoon or the bread.

Move, his brain signaled his shell-shocked muscles.

"Sorry," he said, collecting the items.

She barely waited for him to sit down before she dug into the stew with gusto. She briefly closed her eyes and a blissful expression crossed her delicate features. It reminded him of the sated way she used to look after they'd had sex.

"Mmm, I'd forgotten how good home-cooked food can taste." She licked stew from her bottom lip, and his gut clenched. "It almost makes me regret that I hardly ever cook."

Concentrate on what she's saying, not on those lips and that tongue, all of which he knew from experience could be very clever.

"Why don't you cook more?" he asked.

Her shoulders rose and fell in a shrug that he got the feeling she'd tried to make seem casual. "I guess it's because I made dinner for my family starting from the time I was eleven or twelve."

"That's young to have that kind of responsibility," he said. His mother, who fancied herself a chef, had done the cooking in their family. He hadn't realized steak Diane and chicken Cordon Bleu weren't staples of every family's diet until he'd moved out of the house. "Why didn't your parents do the cooking?"

"Mom's a nurse. She was always working overtime at the hospital. And, Dad, well, Dad was always off somewhere doing God only knew what. And Johnny—that's my brother—is seven years younger than me, so he couldn't help much."

"Didn't your father have a job?"

"Part of the time, but he's never been good about keeping one," she said.

The set of her jaw hinted at a wealth of things left unsaid. He'd gotten the impression the other night that she'd had a difficult phone conversation with her mother. Had there always been this friction in her family? Was it possible it had been there last year, while they'd dated, and he hadn't noticed?

A shutter seemed to come over her face, and she indicated his untouched dinner. "You better eat yours before it gets cold." She paused, tilted her head, narrowed her eyes. "Why are you looking at me like that?"

He took his time in answering. He wanted to know more about her family but sensed she'd said all she would for now. All in due time, he reminded himself, and decided to give her the simple answer. "I guess because I didn't expect this when I opened the door."

"What did you expect?"

"I expected you to demand an apology."

"Because you acted like a jerk? Yeah, you're right. I should ask you to apologize. But, like I said, I'm over it. I mean, it's not like you didn't have my best interests at heart."

"I did?"

"Of course you did. You could tell I wasn't into

Andy, so you tried to make sure I was okay. Why wouldn't I understand that? It's the kind of thing friends do for each other."

"Friends?"

"You still want to be friends, don't you?" She leaned forward as she waited for his answer. Her blouse gaped open slightly, giving him an even better glimpse of her cleavage.

"Sure, I want to be your friend," he said slowly, trying to keep himself from staring at the valley between her breasts. "But I thought you said it wouldn't work."

"I changed my mind." She straightened and took another bite of stew. The tip of her pink tongue flicked out to lick her bottom lip, sending an arrow of heat shooting to his groin. He remembered when that tongue had licked parts of his body, and he had to stifle a moan. "I mean, we're living next door. Why not be friends?"

"I believe your reason was that we're still sexually attracted to each other," he said, his voice thicker than he would have liked. He shifted in his seat, trying to will himself not to get a hard-on. He wasn't successful.

"Oh, that." She waved a hand in the air as though swatting away something as insubstantial as a gnat. "I can get past that if you can. You can, can't you?"

His erection strained against the front of his pants. "Of course," he croaked.

"Good." She rubbed her hands together. "This will be great. I love my girlfriends, but there's something special about being buddies with a guy. Just think of the advice we can give each other."

"Advice about what?"

"The opposite sex, mostly. You might have noticed that I've been dating heavily. I'm serious about finding a guy who's really into me. You can help me with that," she said cheerfully.

Help her find another man to replace him in her bed? He'd never heard a worse plan.

He shook his head. "I'm not a matchmaker."

"I can find my own men," she said. "What I need from you is consultation. Like for the date I have Friday night."

His right hand tightened on his spoon while his left clenched into a fist. "I'm surprised you'd want to go out with Andy again after tonight."

"I'm not going out with Andy," she denied, and his fingers relaxed. "I have a date with somebody else." They clenched again. "We're going to the charity Christmas ball at Hibernian Hall."

Riley knew of the ball. A few months back, he'd even contributed money toward it. The main event was a silent auction, but the evening was an elegant one, punctuated by dancing and fine dining, held at one of the most impressive ballrooms in Charleston.

"Fancy place," he remarked.

"You betcha. Everybody there will be dressed to impress, but the man I'm worried about impressing is my date. That's why I need something new to wear."

"I'm sure you have something in your closet that's good enough," Riley said tightly.

"Not hardly. I need to go shopping, but the thing is, I'm terrible about making decisions like this. So I was wondering if you could meet me over the lunch hour tomorrow at the King Street Boutique."

Every proprietary bone in his body recoiled at helping Kate choose a dress meant to turn the head of another man. "Why don't you ask Julia?"

"*Hello…*" She rolled her eyes. "I need a man's opinion, and Julia's not a man. She can only guess at what men think is sexy. You can tell me. So will you do it?"

He didn't want to. But if he refused, she might think his talk of friendship was nothing more than lip service. And, damn it, he did want to be her friend.

"Sure, I'll help you," he said, forcing himself to smile. "That's what friends are for."

6

KATE BUMPED THE CAR door closed with her hip, holding her cell phone to her ear with one hand and the short, scarlet coat and long, slitted, sapphire skirt earmarked for the dry cleaner with the other.

Wreaths hung from nearby lampposts. Somebody had painted snowflakes and brightly colored ornaments on the window of the nearest storefront. A Salvation Army worker, wearing earmuffs and a smile, rang a bell in front of a red kettle a half block away.

She joined the steady stream of pedestrians on the King Street sidewalk, many of whom carried shopping bags, all the while listening to her mother make excuses for Dad's latest screwup.

She was beginning to think her mother would never stop for air when she took a breath. Kate seized the opportunity to talk sense to her even though it had never worked before.

"No matter how you look at it, Mom, betting on a horse to make up for the money you're not earning is not a good idea."

"But it was a sure thing," her mother said, using

one of Dad's catchphrases. "There was no way the horse could lose."

"Except it did, and now you're worse off than before."

"It's not as though your father meant to put us in this position."

"He never does mean to screw up, Mom, but he always does," Kate interrupted, swaying off her line so as not to get whacked by an oversized M. Dumas & Sons shopping bag. "Can't you see that?"

"I see a man trying his best to do what he thinks is right."

Kate held the receiver out from her mouth so her mother wouldn't hear her heavy sigh, brought it back again and asked, "Bottom line, do you need me to send money?"

"Of course not!" Her mother sounded horror-struck. "Things are a little tight, but they're not dire."

"You're doing extra shifts at the hospital again, aren't you?" Kate asked, even as she spied the dry cleaner's ahead. "That's not a good idea, Mom. Pediatric nursing is stressful. You've got to take care of yourself, and that includes not working so many hours."

"It's only until your father gets another job. He should have one by now. But you know how insecure these bosses can get when someone as qualified as he is applies."

Kate made a face, because she'd heard that excuse the last time Dad had been out of work—and the time before that.

"But enough about your father and me," Mom said. "What's happening with you? Have you given any more thought to that job offer?"

"Not really," Kate said. In truth, she'd forgotten all about the job offer in Philadelphia until just now.

"I hope it's because you're dating someone. I just know you'd be happier with a special man in your life."

"There's nobody," Kate said, which was the problem of the hour. She had two tickets to tomorrow night's charity ball burning a hole in her leopard-print pocketbook. Despite what she'd told Riley, she didn't have a date.

She felt a little guilty about the lie, but he'd made like Pinocchio first. If he'd come straight out and admitted he wanted to sleep with her again instead of spewing that nonsense about friendship, she wouldn't be in this predicament.

She would have told him to stay the hell away from her and that would have been the end of it.

She heard the frown in her mother's voice. "Does your not dating have something to do with that man you gushed over last Christmas?"

"I didn't say I wasn't dating, Mom. Just that I wasn't dating anyone special." Kate hadn't given up hope that some man would gush about *her*. The trick was finding him by tomorrow night. "Believe me, I'm keeping my eyes open."

"Your heart will know the right man when you find him. Mine nearly leaped out of my chest when

I met your father. It still speeds up when he comes into a room, even to this day."

Kate clenched her teeth so she wouldn't tell her mother she'd have been better off if she'd listened to her head.

"Listen, Mom, I've gotta run," she said as she reached the dry cleaner's. "I have errands to do."

"I understand, dear. Now that I have your cell phone number, it will be much easier to reach you. I don't know why I didn't have it before now."

Kate knew. She hadn't wanted to hear her mother tell tales of woe about her father 24/7. Too bad she hadn't shared that sentiment with the Designs on You receptionist, who'd innocently given her mother the number.

Kate clicked off the phone before entering the shop where she'd been a regular since moving to Charleston. A steamy heat wrapped around her, taking the chill out of the day. But she often wondered how Mrs. Gadsden, the proprietress, stood it during the scorching South Carolina summers.

Mrs. Gadsden finished hanging up a bagged garment on the dry-cleaner rack, approached the counter and tore a pink slip off a pad. "When do you need these by, Kate?"

"Anytime next week's fine," Kate said, her attention diverted by a framed photograph she'd never noticed before by the cash register. It depicted a tall, thin man in a crisply starched shirt and knife-creased trousers. Although his face was unlined, his hair was a silvery gray.

"Who's that in the photo?" Kate asked.

"My son," Mrs. Gadsden said proudly.

An idea started to form. "Is he single?"

"Of course he's single."

"Do you think he'd go out with me tomorrow night?"

Deep furrows appeared in Mrs. Gadsden's forehead as she regarded Kate through suspicious eyes. "How old are you?"

"Twenty-six," Kate answered.

"My son's seventeen."

"But his hair…it's gray."

"Prematurely gray." Mrs. Gadsden shook her head. "I'll never understand why some older women think that makes it okay."

"I wouldn't date a teenager!" Kate cried.

Mrs. Gadsden folded her arms over her chest. "I wouldn't let you date him."

"I'd let my son date you."

Kate whirled, surprised that somebody had entered the shop without her noticing. The other customer wore a moss-green coat and a smile on her broad, pleasant face. Kate would have guessed her age at fifty—if she hadn't recently gotten a lesson in how dangerous it was to make assumptions.

"Thank you," Kate said. "I'm sure your son's a perfectly nice boy, but I have to draw the line at dating minors."

"Donald isn't a minor," she said, appearing slightly puzzled. Then she laughed. "Rest assured, he doesn't need my permission to date. He's nearly thirty."

"And unmarried?"

"Regretfully so," the woman said. "I don't understand why some woman hasn't snatched him up. He's handsome, charming and employed. Here, I'll show you a photo."

She dug a slim, black leather wallet from her purse and flipped it open to a photo of a young man with a neatly trimmed beard. His features were perfectly symmetrical, but Kate preferred Riley's slightly crooked smile.

"Donald is a stockbroker. Isn't he handsome? He used to model in college."

A warning bell went off in Kate's head. She didn't have a head for business and was terrible with numbers. What would they talk about?

"Give me your phone number and I'll have him call you," the woman said.

"It's such short notice," Kate said. "The date I need is for tomorrow night. I have tickets to the charity Christmas ball at Hibernian Hall."

"I'll make sure he's free. Now, do you have anything to write with?"

Mrs. Gadsden tore another page off her pink pad and handed it to Kate along with a pen. "As long as you stay away from my baby, I'm all for you going out."

"My son's going to adore you," the other woman added.

Kate tried to smile, telling herself that was what she wanted. A man who adored her.

So why was she looking forward more to buying a dress for her date than the date itself?

"WHAT DO YOU THINK OF this dress?"

Riley folded his arms over his chest from his position in the Queen Anne armchair in the back of the boutique and pretended to give the matter great thought.

Kate stood before him in the fourth of four little red dresses she'd taken into the dressing room to try on.

This dress had all of the features that had made breathing so difficult over the past fifteen minutes. The neckline showcased her cleavage. The material clung like a second layer of skin. The hemline revealed far more leg than it concealed.

All in all, not a dress he'd prefer Kate wear on a date with another man. None of the other three had been, either, with the possible exception of the first. Either the dresses were getting sexier or he was getting more and more turned on.

"It's a nice dress, but maybe not exactly what you're looking for," he said.

"Are you sure?" She examined herself critically in the mirror, smoothing her hands over the material from the swell of her breasts down to the curve of her hips. Damn, she had a hot body. His stomach tightened. "I think this might be the dress to drop Donald's jaw."

Riley gritted his teeth so he wouldn't say something unflattering about Donald, not that he knew anything about the guy aside from the fact that he shared his name with a duck.

"I think the first dress might have been sexier." He hoped he sounded like a fashion consultant giving sage advice instead of a man lying through his teeth.

"You really think so? I guess I could try it on again."

"How are we doing?" The saleswoman appeared from the front of the shop, using the falsely cheerful voice she probably reserved for customers. She was one of those tall, ultra-thin blondes who inspired envy in women who worried about their weight but who men thought should eat more.

"I'm not sure," Kate said, still scrutinizing herself in the mirror. "What do you think of this dress? I want something knock-your-socks-off sexy, but Riley isn't sure this is it."

The saleswoman arched eyebrows significantly darker than her ash-blond hair. "If you're looking for sexy, do I have the dress for you."

She swept away but returned in seconds, holding out a dress that was barely there even when draped on a hanger. Riley could see through parts of a garment that featured the stretchy, second-skin type of material popular in running tights.

"Try this on," the saleswoman said with a smug air.

Kate eagerly took the skimpy material masquerading as a dress, and disappeared into the dressing room. A bell signaled, indicating another customer had entered the shop.

The saleslady excused herself, and Riley settled deeper in his chair and thought about the car engine he'd rebuilt as a teenager. He mentally went over the steps, the same way he had the other times she'd changed clothes. The trick got his mind off how hot she looked in the dresses and how he'd like to be in that dressing room with her, seeing her in nothing at all.

"Riley, are you out there? I'm having trouble with the zipper."

He bolted upright, leaving the alternator hovering over the engine, imagining her half dressed.

"I'll see if the saleslady can come help," he offered.

"Can't you do it?" Her question stopped him. The door to the dressing room cracked open, and she looked out with her big, almond-shaped eyes. "Please."

He swallowed and gave the only response he seemed capable of making. "Okay."

"Come on in, then." She disappeared into the dressing room, making it clear she expected him to join her. But was there room enough in there for both of them? He hesitated.

"Riley?" she called. "Are you coming?"

He rubbed his forehead at her unfortunate choice of words and willed his penis to behave. Putting one foot in front of the other, he slipped through the crack.

She stood before a full-length mirror, the red dress barely covering the front of her body. Her back was bare from her neck to the swell of her rear end, and a skimpy bra she'd discarded sat on top of the clothes she'd piled on a corner chair.

She met his eyes in the mirror. "Zip me up, please?" she asked, her voice sounding husky.

He bit down on his teeth so he wouldn't moan, and moved forward a step—all the space he had. His palms felt damp and his fingers clumsy as he reached for her zipper and encountered warm, sleek, bare skin.

He held his breath so it wouldn't feel hot and uneven on her neck as he anchored his left hand at the small of her back and tugged the zipper slowly upward. Her eyes watched his throughout the entire journey.

"Thank you," she said when he was through.

"You're welcome," he breathed, his eyes still locked on her mirrored ones.

"Riley?"

The dressing room was too small to hide anything, including the electricity humming between them. Surely she felt that. Would she admit to it?

"Yeah."

"You can let go of the zipper now." She flashed him an easy smile. "And move so I can get out of here and see what the dress looks like."

The spell broken, his hands dropped to his sides. He backed up quickly, banging an elbow against the wall of the dressing room in his haste to leave the small space.

The air outside the cubicle felt cooler, but immediately heated back up when she stepped out of the dressing room.

Afraid she'd notice the effect their interlude with the zipper had had on his body, he backed up until his legs hit the chair. He sank into it and immediately folded his hands in his lap.

When he looked at her, he had to clamp his teeth together to prevent his jaw from dropping. This was the punishment he got for trying to dissuade her from buying the other dress. Kate in this dress could cause a riot in a community of monks.

The garment clung tantalizingly to every one of her ample curves without making it seem like she were auditioning for a pinup calendar. The designer had added demure touches—peekaboo lace at the neckline and a skirt that flared around the thighs—that made the dress even more provocative.

"Now there's a sexy dress." The saleswoman appeared, clapping her hands together. "There aren't many woman who have the figure to wear it, but you do."

"What do you think, Riley?" Kate came toward him on the sexy red heels she'd worn with every dress, smoothing the material over her bustline and down her hips as she walked.

He couldn't make his throat work over the thickness that had settled there. Kate leaned over his chair, putting so much gorgeous body on display, he thought he might have a heart attack.

"Riley?" she pressed.

"It's, um, quite a dress," Riley said, certain he didn't want to send Kate off into the world wearing it.

"You don't sound enthusiastic," Kate said with a little frown. Could she possibly not know how amazing she looked? "Do you still like the first one better?"

He didn't, of course. This was the dress that could drive a man wild. The room temperature had spiked substantially since he'd looked at her in it. He didn't imagine Donald's reaction would be any different.

"You look ten times sexier in this dress than the other one," the saleslady interjected. "I'm sure your boyfriend agrees."

"He's not my boyfriend," Kate said. "He's my friend."

Friend.

The word intruded on Riley's conscience. He'd insisted to Kate that he wanted to be her friend, and she'd finally given him the chance to be exactly that.

What kind of a friend would he be if she asked for his advice and he lied to her?

"She's right. You look gorgeous." He no longer bothered to hide his naked appreciation. Her lips curved into a wide smile that made her even more irresistible. "Donald won't be able to take his eyes off you."

Or his hands.

His gut clenched again, but this time it wasn't from sexual frustration.

KATE SWITCHED ON HER bedroom light, kicked off her strappy ruby-red heels and shimmied out of her sexy crimson dress before collapsing on her bed.

She sprawled on her back, staring at her ceiling. In a fit of romantic whimsy, she'd painted blue and gold stars in the form of the constellation Pegasus. In Greek mythology, Pegasus was the horse on which Perseus flew to rescue the beautiful maiden, Andromeda, from the sea monster.

But there were no stars in Kate's eyes tonight.

Oh, the atmosphere at the charity ball had been glitzy, the food delicious and the crowd decked out in sparkles and formal wear. Not only that, her come-hither dress had been a major success.

With the notable exception of her handsome, charming date, she'd been hit on by no less than five men.

Hadn't Riley foreseen that men would flock to her when he'd recommended she buy the sexiest dress in all of Charleston?

Hadn't he even cared?

Perseus wouldn't have sent Andromeda off into the Greek countryside wearing a little scrap of nothing that might inspire other men to slay monsters for her.

But then, nothing in Greek mythology said that Perseus and Andromeda had been in a relationship that was all about sex.

No matter what Riley said about friendship, the visit to the boutique proved he still viewed Kate as a sex object.

She'd watched Riley squirm during the private

fashion show. She'd felt his warm, strong hands linger when he'd helped with her zipper. She'd seen the strain on his face as he fought not to act on the attraction.

For fleeting moments, she'd felt a surge of feminine triumph that Riley still desired her.

Then, after all that, he'd told the truth about which dress was sexiest. The truth!

The phone rang, sounding unnaturally loud in the quiet of her bedroom. The iridescent red numbers on her bedside clock showed it was well past eleven.

Nobody called this late except her mother, who thought Kate should be available whenever she needed to talk. But who said Kate couldn't talk to her mother when she needed *her?* Mom, after all, knew about the many ways a man could disappoint.

She rolled over on her bed so that she was on her stomach, snatched up the receiver and said hello.

"Hey, Kate. I hope it's not too late to call." Riley's deep voice rumbled through her, making it feel as though he was in the bedroom with her instead of an apartment away. "I wanted to see how it went."

How had he expected it to go after sending her out into the world dressed like a man-magnet?

"How do you know I'm alone?" she asked, barely managing to bank her temper.

"Because you don't bring a guy back to your place on the first date."

"I did you," she reminded him.

Silence followed, and she realized he could have viewed her response as a double entendre. She felt her face heat. "I meant to say, things between us moved pretty fast."

"I know what you meant, but I like to think those were special circumstances." His low, soft voice wrapped around her like the silk sheets she used on her bed when she wanted to pamper herself.

Her temper faded but didn't vanish. He'd chosen the come-get-me dress, but she had to give him points for knowing she wasn't promiscuous. Unless, of course, he'd looked out the window and seen her return by herself. She frowned, stacked one of her pillows on top of the other, then sat up so her back rested against the headboard.

"You're right," she admitted. "I'm alone."

An obnoxious blaring came over the line. She held the phone out from her ear but the noise lasted mere seconds.

"Sorry," Riley said. "I was setting my alarm for to-morrow morning and it went off."

"Are you in bed?"

"Yep, I'm in bed."

Unwelcome warmth spread through her as she pictured his hard body naked, the way he liked to sleep. Or did he? They'd never done much sleeping when they were together. He could prefer boxer shorts and a T-shirt, for all she knew.

"So was the dress a hit?" he asked.

The dress. She wasted a good scowl, considering he couldn't see it. He wanted to hear about the dress? Fine, she'd tell him.

"Is Christmas in December?" she asked.

"I take it that's a yes," he said, and she couldn't read anything in his voice, let alone disappointment or jealousy. "Tell me about it."

"Let's see. We hadn't been there ten minutes when Donald ran into a woman he'd gone to high school with. While she and Donald caught up on old times, her husband told me I reminded him of a tamale and asked for my phone number."

"Tacky."

"Another guy waited until his date was in the rest room to say I looked so hot I must be the reason for global warming. And, oh yes, another wanted me to put him out of his misery by going back to his hotel room with him."

"What about Donald? What did he say?"

She hesitated, thinking about how to word her answer without revealing what she'd learned about Donald. "He's quite the gentleman. He said he was honored to be at the ball with such a beautiful woman."

"So you like him?"

The question sounded innocent enough, like something one of her girlfriends might ask.

"Of course I like him," she said. "He's handsome, charming, witty, funny. An all-around good guy."

"He must've been disappointed to have the evening end like it did."

She wondered why Riley would ask such a leading question after encouraging her to wear a dress like that.

"I wouldn't say that he was disappointed, exactly," she hedged.

"Aw, come on." His disbelief was audible. "I saw you in that dress, Kate. A man would have to be crazy not to want you."

She wanted to ask if that included him, but of course it must. She believed in monogamy. She'd never become sexually involved with a man who was dating somebody else. But maybe Riley had different standards.

She rubbed her forehead, which had started to ache from trying to figure out the meaning behind his words. She couldn't do this anymore. Not tonight.

"Listen, Riley, it's late and I'm tired. Can we continue this conversation tomorrow?"

"I have to work tomorrow."

"Me, too," she said.

"Do you want to meet for dinner?"

"I might not be finished by then. I'm doing the interiors for a couple who work long hours during the week so they want to get everything done on Saturday," she said. "Why don't we play it by ear? I'll see you tomorrow, okay?"

"Tomorrow," he said softly, the word sounding like a promise.

She hung up the phone and punched her pillow, making a promise of her own.

Tomorrow she'd get Riley to admit what he really wanted from her. She just needed to figure out a way to do it.

7

How had he gotten himself roped into this? Riley wondered as Kate arranged herself in a cross-legged position on her living room floor.

It had started innocently enough with a knock on his door and another big-eyed plea for help.

What could he say but yes?

But before he'd agreed, he should have found out why she was decked out in a white spandex tank top and pink spandex shorts.

He shouldn't have worried that uttering more than a syllable of agreement could have left his tongue in danger of hanging out.

"You're a doll for helping me out like this, Riley." Kate smiled up at him and he tried hard to focus on her face rather than her breasts. He even half succeeded. "I've been so stiff all day, and you can't do these stretching exercises without a partner."

"What should I do?"

"Stand behind me, bend your knees slightly and press them into my upper back."

He did as she asked, positioning his knees against her sleek, muscular back. A current ran through him, firing his nerve endings, which was strange considering the knees weren't typically considered an erogenous zone.

"That's good." She extended her arms to the sides, bent them ninety degrees at the elbow and pointed her hands toward the ceiling. "Now put your hands on my upper arms and gently pull back. It's supposed to stretch the chest and shoulders."

If given a choice, her arms wouldn't be where he'd choose to put his hands. But he still enjoyed the feel of her smooth, warm skin under his fingers.

"Aah, that feels good." She arched her back and thrust out her breasts so that he could see the outline of her nipples. "A little lower. Yes, that's the spot. Umm. That's wonderful."

He felt beads of sweat form above his upper lip. Why did it sound like she was talking about sex? Why was he even thinking about it? Sex and his got-to-have-it-now libido had gotten him into trouble in the first place.

"Let's try another position," she said. "My hamstring's really tight."

So were the front of his pants. He released her, and she lay on her back with her arms flung overhead and her legs extended. Her breasts rose and fell in a regular rhythm, and she wore a satisfied expression.

She raised one of her legs straight up while keeping the other flat against the floor.

"For this stretch, I need you to get in front of me and gently press my raised leg toward my face."

She had to be kidding. That leg was temptation incarnate. The spandex shorts hugged her firm thigh, and her shapely calf was bare.

"Riley?" she prompted when he didn't move. "Is something wrong?"

"No." He surreptitiously cleared his throat when the denial came off sounding too husky. "Everything's fine."

He circled around and knelt in front of her, putting both hands on her raised leg. The skin on her calf was smooth, as though she'd shaved that morning. He fought the impulse to trace her sleek muscles and hoped she didn't notice his palms were damp.

"You're good at this," she said after he'd helped her stretch out both hamstrings and her quadriceps.

She sat up. Pieces of her hair stuck out from her head even more haphazardly than usual. Her face was free of makeup. She looked gorgeous.

"And to think I almost told you I didn't want to be friends. You are such a better friend than you are a boyfriend."

His heart nearly thudded to a stop. Had he messed up here? Should he have admitted before now that he wanted to be both her friend and lover?

"Can you believe I actually thought the friendship thing was a ploy to get me back in your bed?"

He strived to sound surprised. "No?"

"Yes, I did. And how can you blame me after the way you kissed me that night?"

"You mean the night you kissed me back?"

"I did, didn't I?" She rolled her eyes. "Silly me for

thinking about messing up the beginning of a beautiful friendship."

She jumped to her feet. He was still on his knees, in prime exercise partner position. He should get up, but he couldn't be sure his pants wouldn't tent.

"Wait for me while I take a shower, okay? We never did finish that talk we started last night, and I'm in need of dating advice."

She started toward the bathroom, her spandex-clad rear end swaying provocatively. He barely lifted his eyes in time when she turned around and hurried back toward him.

"Oh, and thanks for helping me stretch."

Without warning, she bent over and kissed him. On the cheek.

"Don't go anywhere," she said, then disappeared into the bathroom.

He stared after her, feeling the warm imprint of her lips where she'd kissed him. He should feel elated that his plan had worked.

But now that they were well on their way to being friends, how in the hell could he convince her to be his lover without having his motives questioned?

He shut his eyes tight and rubbed his forehead. He should be grateful that her comment had stopped him from stating his true intentions. They'd only begun to get reacquainted.

He took a deep breath, strengthening his resolve not to rush her into bed and saying a silent thank you to Kate for reminding him of the importance of friendship.

KATE WIPED A SECTION of steam off the bathroom mirror with the edge of the towel she'd used to dry her hair.

She finger-combed the dark strands until they fell in artful disarray, then adjusted the skinny straps of the low-cut tank top she'd paired with sleep pants decorated with Andy Warhol paintings.

The tank top was black, loose-fitting and skimpy enough to make clear she wasn't wearing a bra.

"Good." She addressed her braless image in the mirror while smoothing her hands over her breasts. "Let's see him pretend to ignore these babies."

He hadn't done a very good job of masking his feelings thus far. His face had been strained while he helped her through the stretching exercises. When his voice had cracked, she'd almost felt sorry for him.

Almost, but not quite.

Okay, maybe she was laying the temptation on a bit thick with the sexy red dresses, the spandex and the bra-free breasts.

But she hadn't asked Riley to do anything she wouldn't ask of a girlfriend.

Girlfriends helped you shop, held your feet while you stretched and thought nothing of seeing you braless. If all Riley truly wanted was friendship, none of that would phase him.

"Ha," she said to the mirror. "Like I believe that for a second."

She pasted on a friendly smile and emerged from

the bathroom on bare feet. She found Riley in the den, examining an object in his hands.

"Sorry I took so long," she said to announce her presence.

His head came up, his jaw went slack and his eyes zeroed in. He didn't say a word. Gotcha.

"Riley?"

"Yeah?"

"You're staring."

"Sorry." His eyes dropped from her breasts. "Those are some pants."

So he wanted her to think he'd been staring at her pants? Fat chance. But, hey, two could play this game. She kicked up a leg.

"Aren't they great? I got them at an art museum. They kind of match the place, don't you think?"

She'd decorated the apartment with a complete disregard for the old-world exterior. The place was a haven for funky furniture, splashy artwork, wild wallpaper borders and gaily colored accent walls.

"You're the only woman I know who could pull off wearing those pants," he said.

She noticed that the item he'd been examining was a photo frame shaped like a miniature television set and made of red rubber. She gestured at it.

"That's a photo of me, my mom and my brother, Johnny. I gave my mom one of those same frames last Christmas. I told her it was because she's pretty enough to be on TV."

"She is. You look like her, especially around the eyes and mouth," he said, and her heart warmed at the compliment. "But I don't see a resemblance with your brother. Does he take after your Dad?'

"Only in looks," she said, something she gave thanks for with regularity. "Johnny's a good kid. He's a senior in high school but already has a scholarship to Temple. He's going to major in engineering."

"Is your father an engineer, too?"

She bit back her bark of laughter. "Not hardly."

"What does he do, then?"

"Not much of anything except bullshit my mom," she retorted before she could edit her answer. She shook her head. "I'm sorry. I shouldn't have said that, but my Dad's a sore spot."

"Is that why you don't have a photo of him on display?"

She'd brushed Riley off a few nights ago when he'd asked about her father, but found herself answering this time. "I honestly didn't realize I didn't have a photo of him. But we're not close, if that's what you're asking."

"Why not?"

"Let's just say I can see through him, which is something my mother has never managed. She'd be a lot better off without him."

"Does she think so?"

"That's the thing. She doesn't," Kate said on a sigh. "Can we talk about something else. I've got a surprise for you."

She left the living room, shaking her head and chastising herself for opening up to him. She'd asked him over to tempt him, not to confide in him.

"I have ice cream," she announced when she re-joined him, indicating the quart-size carton she carried. "Häagen-Dazs chocolate raspberry torte."

She padded over to the sofa and plopped down inches from him, so he'd be able to look down her top if he turned his head.

He turned his head.

She smiled to herself at his quick indrawn breath. Any day now, he'd crack. Maybe even tonight. Prying off the lid of the ice-cream carton, she handed him one of two spoons.

"We can share," she said before she dug in and scooped up a bite. The creamy chocolate melted in her mouth.

"Mmm, good." She licked the remnants of chocolate from her lips, then asked with big-eyed pseudo-innocence, "Want some?"

He swallowed hard, causing his Adam's apple to bob, and female satisfaction burst inside her.

"Yes," he said after long, pregnant moments. "I do."

He turned his body sideways, edging a few inches farther away from her in the process, and helped himself to some ice cream. This time, when he licked chocolate from his lips, she was the one who squirmed.

She blinked, disconcerted by her reaction. She'd been so busy trying to be a temptress that she'd failed to notice how hot he looked tonight.

Not hot in his usual young, successful business-man sort of way, but Charleston casual hot. A day's worth of beard darkened his lower face. He wore sweatpants, thick, white athletic socks and a faded

Spoleto Festival T-shirt that didn't hide the muscle definition in his arms.

"So you were going to tell me more about last night," he said. "You never did say why Donald wasn't disappointed that your date ended early."

She thought about how to answer without completely giving away the secret she'd discovered about Donald. "Not every man wants sex from a woman on the first date."

"I disagree." He reached into the carton to scoop more ice cream. "Some men are better at hiding it, but that doesn't mean they're not thinking about it."

"That's not true!"

"Sure is." He ate another bite of ice cream. "Believe me. Donald thought about sex last night when he looked at you."

"I know he didn't."

"Then he must be gay."

"So what if he is?"

The moment the retort was out of her mouth, she wanted to take it back. But she couldn't, not when he was looking at her with furrowed brows.

"Donald's gay?"

She sighed. So much for leading her ex-boyfriend to believe she had another man lined up to take his place. "A word of advice—don't accept a date if the mother's the one arranging it."

"A date with the sexiest woman in Charleston and he's gay!" Laughter and something else—was that relief?—mingled in his voice.

She ignored the frisson of satisfaction she got from

his comment and concentrated on his gloating. "I believe we've already established that Donald's gay," she said in a dry voice.

"But I don't get it. Why did Donald's mother set you up with her gay son?"

"She doesn't know he's gay."

"He hasn't told her?"

"He says his mother couldn't handle it. Personally, I think he's selling her short. Especially because his lover is such a doll."

"You met his lover? This gets better and better." He grinned at her. "Wait a minute. Let me guess. His lover came on the date with you."

Finally seeing the humor in the situation, she let a smile break free. She giggled, tucked her legs under her, put the ice-cream carton and her spoon on the nearest table and angled her body toward him.

"No, he didn't come with us, smart aleck. I didn't feel comfortable with Donald picking me up, so I offered to drive."

"Hey, if you'd told me it was a blind date, I would have checked out the guy for you." His expression was earnest, the offer no doubt sincere.

"That's what Donald's boyfriend did to me. Donald wasn't ready yet when I got there so he sat me down and quizzed me. I thought he was just being nosy."

"How did you find out Donald was gay?"

"Let's see." She pretended to think. "I had a pretty good idea when his roommate kissed him goodbye. On the lips."

When Riley chuckled, she picked up her spoon and rapped him lightly on the upper arm. "It's not funny. There I was in the sexiest dress I've ever owned trying to look hot for a gay man."

"I'm sure he appreciated the effort," he said between laughs.

"Oh, he did. Donald's actually a very nice man. He felt so bad about the misunderstanding that he's setting me up with a friend he promises is heterosexual."

Riley stopped laughing. "Another blind date? Are you sure you want to do that?"

"Why not? It's as good a way as any to meet someone."

"But you can't be too cautious these days." He lightly tapped his chin with his fist, appearing deep in thought. "When are you two going out?"

"Tomorrow night," she answered slowly.

"If I could manage to get a date, we could double."

"That's not such a good idea," she instantly refuted, then thought about what he'd said. "You actually think you'd have trouble getting a date?"

"Well, yeah. It's pretty short notice."

"Like that will be a problem for you." She rolled her eyes. "Just call the number on the back of the business card that saleslady gave you yesterday."

He regarded her closely. "You knew about that?"

She shrugged, determined not to let him know that the other woman hitting on him had bothered her. "She wasn't exactly circumspect."

"I guess not, but I'm not going to call her."

"You're not attracted to her? But she's beautiful."

"She's not my type," he said, which had started to sound like a familiar refrain.

"So who would you ask?" she asked, forgetting, for the moment, that she hadn't agreed to a double date.

"I'm thinking Lana."

"Julia's friend from the bar?"

"We got along fine. I bet she'd do this for me as a favor."

A favor? Didn't he think Lana would jump at the chance to go out with him?

"So what do you say?" he asked. "Me and Lana, you and Donald's non-gay friend?"

Having her ex-lover along when another man was auditioning to be his replacement sounded dreadful. "I'm not that paranoid about going on a blind date."

"Then indulge me." He took her hand, which was still cold from holding the ice-cream carton, and squeezed it gently, instantly warming it. "I'd worry about you all evening if I didn't come along. This way, I'll know you're fine."

His dark brown eyes had turned so soft, they reminded her of chocolate left out in the sun. Her resistance melted, too.

"You'd really worry about me?" she asked in a soft voice.

"I really would," he said.

"Okay, then," she whispered back. "It's a double date."

8

RILEY ENJOYED THE STEADY stream of jazz from the baby grand piano in the corner of the bar, especially because it wasn't obtrusive enough to interfere with the conversation at the table.

"How could you not like the play? Didn't you think the notion of stealing Christmas was intriguing?" Riley challenged.

"It's been done before," Kate said with a toss of her head. She pointed a finger at him. "And when the Grinch did it, it wasn't so boring."

They'd come to the piano bar after watching a production of *Where in the World is St. Nick?* at the Dock Street Theater, an architectural treasure in the heart of downtown Charleston.

"It wasn't boring! Nick's wife and kids had no idea he'd take all the money and run after he sat in for Santa at the mall. It looked like one of the elves had offed him."

"I figured out the elf was too stupid to be a criminal mastermind before the end of Act One. It was hard to sit through the rest of it. Talk, talk, talk. That's all those characters did."

Riley snorted in disbelief, but in reality he was enjoying the debate. "What did you want them to do? Go Hollywood and destroy the furniture on stage? It wasn't an action movie."

"Now you're talking." She grinned at him. "I'm a child of the nineties. I love that kind of stuff."

"Me, too," interjected Tony Quaglio. "I'd take Steven Spielberg over a Christmas mystery any day."

"Not me," Lana Murphy said. "I miss the days when movies bothered to set the stage before they blew it up."

Until Tony and Lana had spoken, Riley had almost forgotten that he and Kate were on a double date. Almost, but not quite.

Tony, with his Italian Romeo good looks and hooded dark eyes, was impossible to overlook. So was Tony's right arm, which he'd kept around Kate's seat back for the duration of the play. Riley had overheard him apologize to Kate, explaining that the fat man on his opposite side was crowding him. But the fat man was nowhere in sight now, and Tony's arm rested on the back of yet another of Kate's chairs.

Riley felt something on his own arm and glanced down at the long fingers of Lana's left hand. She leaned close to him.

"I guess it's me and you against Kate and Tony," Lana said, then addressed the other two. "It's hard to believe you two only just met. You're like two peas in a pot."

"I think you mean two peas in a *pod*," Tony said, slanting Lana a good-natured smile.

"That is what I meant." Lana squeezed Riley's arm when she laughed, and he felt the sharp half moons of her claw-like fingernails through his clothes. "I can't believe how alike you two are."

"I don't think they're alike," Riley said.

"Then you haven't been paying attention." Lana laughed again. Why did she keep doing that? What was so funny anyway? "They're both from Philadelphia, they both have Italian ancestry and they both don't like to sit still."

"I've been thinking the same thing." This time, Tony sent that beaming, Latin-lover smile Kate's way. "I owe Donald a beer—hell, a case of beer—for giving me Kate's number."

"I hear you," Lana said to Tony but squeezed Riley's arm. He'd have bruises by the time the night was over. "Sometimes you just click with somebody."

The piano player switched to a different tune. Lana's nose wrinkled and her lips pouted. "You'd never tell it was less than two weeks before Christmas by the songs this guy is playing. We should request something festive."

"He's playing something festive right now." Riley could identify most jazz favorites but at the moment his concentration was shot. "Give me a minute and I'll tell you the name of the song."

"'Boogie Woogie Santa Clause,'" Kate supplied triumphantly.

Riley raised his beer mug in salute. "A woman after my own heart."

Take that, Tony Quaglio, he wanted to add. Only two people at the table would have a chance at a jazz version of *Name That Tune,* and Tony wasn't one of them.

"I'd rather hear a traditional version of 'Jingle Bells' or 'White Christmas,'" Lana complained. "But right now I need to go to the ladies' room. Kate, come with me?"

"I'm fine." Kate waved her off. "You go ahead without me."

Not five seconds later, Kate reversed her answer. Lana got up first, waiting for Kate to join her. When she did, Riley found it surprising that the older woman had three or four inches on Kate. Kate claimed the attention whenever the two of them were in the same room, which made her seem taller.

He watched Kate follow Lana to the rest room, smiling at her wild, purple minidress and matching high-heeled boots. When he'd commented on the color, she'd claimed the dress wasn't purple, but mulberry.

"How long have you and Kate known each other?" Tony asked when the two women were out of sight. Tony had obviously watched Kate's retreat, too.

"A little over a year now. Why?"

"Just wondering." The space between his eyes narrowed. "You seem...close."

"We're friends," Riley said, and realized that's what they were becoming. Exactly the way he'd planned.

"Really?" Tony slanted him an assessing look. "You must be a real good friend. I got the impression you were along tonight to check me out."

"I didn't realize it was that obvious." Riley looked the other man directly in the eyes. Tony unflinchingly returned the stare.

"So what do you think?"

Riley reached for his beer and took a long pull so he could delay his answer. He'd only been partially honest with Kate about why he wanted to come along tonight. His main goal had been to break up a romance before it began.

But now that he thought about it, Lana was right. He and Kate might share a love of jazz, but Tony had a lot more in common with Kate than a southern boy who took things slowly. If Kate really liked this guy, how could he stand in the way?

"I think you seem like a good guy," Riley finally said.

Tony lifted his beer mug and grinned. "I'll drink to that."

Riley drank, too, but he had a hard time swallowing the brew past the lump in his throat.

KATE BENT OVER THE porcelain sink to get closer to the rest room mirror, spread her lips and got an eyeful of white teeth.

She frowned. Could she have misinterpreted Lana's signal back at the table when she'd met Kate's eyes, briefly bared her teeth and pointed between two of them?

"I don't see anything between my teeth," she said to Lana, who was digging a tube of lipstick from her purse.

"Sorry about that." Lana looked anything but. Her pretty dark eyes sparkled. "I needed to get you alone. I want to make sure it's okay with you if I move in on Riley."

Somehow Kate kept her mouth from dropping open and her heart from stopping.

"When we first met, I thought you and Riley might be a couple." Lana stopped talking to put on a layer of sienna-colored lipstick. "But then Riley asked me out tonight, and I figured maybe I was wrong."

"About Riley and me being a couple?"

"About you two lusting after each other." She laughed and shook her head. "That was my imagination, right? You and Riley, you're just friends?"

Lana made friendship sound trivial, as though it couldn't stand in the way of a good romance.

Seemingly oblivious that Kate had yet to respond, Lana continued, "Because one thing I don't do is move in on another woman's man. Tell me to back off, and I will."

Could it really be so easy? *Back off,* Kate wanted to shout. But what if Lana relayed her comment to Riley?

"I can't tell you that," Kate said slowly.

"Then it's true you two are just friends?"

Kate swallowed. That's what Riley said he wanted to be. Even though Kate's motives hadn't been pure, that's what she'd agreed to.

"Yes," she said. "We're friends."

"What a huge relief." Lana clasped her hands together and beamed. "Then I'm going for it."

A sick feeling spread in Kate's stomach. Lana's black dress wasn't as sexy as the one Kate had worn to the charity ball, but it clung nicely to her curves. She was an attractive woman. Riley might not be able to resist her.

"You sure you want to do that? I think Riley considers you a friend, too."

"Not a problem." Lana grinned at her and giggled. "Once I have my hands on him, he'll figure out soon enough that I'm in the market for more than friendship."

Lana used those hands to start conveying her message when they returned to the table. She constantly ran them over Riley's arm, caressed his hand and found excuses to touch him.

Kate's mind played a trick on her, transporting her back a year ago to when she'd walked into that restaurant and seen Elle Dumont and Riley sharing that kiss. Only this time, in her mind's eye, the woman wasn't Elle. It was Lana.

Kate's stomach rolled. She couldn't sit here any longer, watching Lana make the moves on a man her heart had once considered hers. She opened her mouth to call it a night but Lana spoke first.

"Riley, would you mind terribly if we left?" she asked in a sugary sweet tone, her eyelashes batting, her hand clinging to his arm.

Riley looked across the table at Kate, as though

asking for…permission to leave? But could that be? Did Kate really have any say in whether Riley took off with Lana?

"It depends on Kate," he said, and the breath she'd been holding left her lungs. Of course. How had his reason for insisting on the double date slipped her mind? He wouldn't leave until he was sure she felt comfortable being left alone with Tony.

"You two go ahead," she said with a forced smile. Far be it from her to admit she didn't want to spend time with Tony when Riley had no qualms about leaving with Lana. "Tony and I are still enjoying the evening, aren't we, Tony?"

"Definitely," Tony said.

Riley hesitated only slightly before he stood, then leaned across the table so that his face was close to hers. She could pick out flecks of midnight in his brown eyes and feel his warm breath on her face when he whispered, "He's a good guy, Kate."

Then he straightened and, with Lana clinging to him and laughing about something, walked out of the bar. Kate watched him go in stunned silence. Riley glanced back over his shoulder when he reached the exit, but she quickly broke eye contact and focused on Tony.

He's a good guy, Kate, Riley had said. What the hell had that meant? Had *he* been giving *her* permission to do God knew what with Tony?

"You look like you could use another drink," Tony said.

"I could at that," she said gratefully.

He signaled a waiter, who brought her a whiskey sour, and then proceeded to try to get to know her better. Concentrating very hard on shoving Riley from her mind, Kate discovered that Lana was right.

She and Tony did have many things in common, from their Philadelphia backgrounds to the competitive streaks that ran thickly through them.

"I let you win at darts tonight. You know that, don't you?" Tony said later as he walked her to her car.

"I know a lie when I hear one, that's what I know," she retorted, and he threw back his head and laughed.

She'd parked in an outdoor lot in an area of downtown Charleston that usually boasted a heavy horse-and-buggy trade, but the horses and their drivers had called it a night hours ago. Even though it wasn't that late, they were the only two people in the parking lot.

"You sure you're okay to drive?" Tony asked when they reached her Toyota Spyder.

"Let's see. Two drinks in two hours? Yeah, I'm sure." She smiled at him and he gave her a winning smile in return that accentuated his dark good looks. She willed her heart to speed up, but it wouldn't cooperate. "Thank you for a lovely evening."

"You're welcome."

She'd let him kiss her, she decided. Why not? Riley was off with Lana, and Tony had made it clear he was interested. Tony had good looks and intelligence going for him. Her mother would say he was quite the catch. Even Riley approved of him.

Tony dipped his head, she raised her lips, and he deposited a very dry, very chaste kiss on her lips.

"I wish things had turned out differently," he said when he straightened. "He's one lucky guy."

"Who is?"

"Riley Carter." He raised a hand in farewell and walked away.

"Lucky guy, you say?" Kate fumed to herself ten minutes later as she trudged up the stairs to her apartment. Why did everybody keep assuming she and Riley had something going on? Yes, she'd had a thing for him once, but she'd worked hard to overcome it.

Even if remnants of those feelings remained, she didn't intend to act on them. Riley had obviously moved on. Why else had he gone out of his way to tell her Tony was a good guy?

"A good guy," she muttered darkly. "The nerve of him to say a thing like that."

Who cared if it were the truth? Who cared if it were what a friend would say? She'd already established that it was sex, and not friendship, that Riley wanted from her.

Then why had he tried to pawn her off on another man? Had Riley given up on trying to be her lover as soon as another willing woman had come along?

And if he had, well…how dare he!

His car was parked on the street, but Lana could very well be with him right now.

Kate stood very still in the hall between her apartment and Riley's and listened, but she couldn't hear anything except the slight creaking of the old building.

How would she get to sleep tonight without knowing if Lana had succeeded in seducing Riley? But short of knocking on Riley's door, how would she know if Lana was inside his apartment?

She stuck her door key in the lock, but inspiration struck before she could turn it.

Without pausing to examine her reasons behind the idea, she removed the key and tucked it in her jacket pocket. Then she marched to Riley's door and knocked.

A good twenty seconds passed. She was about to rap again when the door swung open.

Riley stood there in the same clothes he'd worn earlier tonight, except his shirt was untucked, his hair was mussed and his long, well-shaped feet were bare.

"Kate," he said, running a hand through his hair. "I thought you'd still be out with Tony."

"Oh, really." She drew out the syllables, irked that he was still trying to foist her on the other man. "You'd like that, wouldn't you? With him being such a good guy and all."

He blinked. "Excuse me?"

"You said Tony was a good guy, right?"

"Yes," he admitted slowly.

"There you have it," she said, because that explained it all. "But I'm not here to argue with you." She raised her hands in a gesture she hoped looked sheepish. "I locked myself out."

She cocked her head, waiting to see if he'd invite her in. He didn't. She peered over his shoulder but couldn't tell whether he was alone. "Can I come in?"

He hesitated. "Okay," he said after a moment, and stepped back.

Her eyes roamed over the heavy, dark furniture and brown-and-beige color scheme of an apartment in desperate need of an interior decorator. But she didn't mentally redo the apartment, as she so often did when faced with something lacking in style. She had a more important mission.

"Does anybody have your spare?" he asked.

"My spare what?" she asked while checking the living room and kitchen. Empty.

"Your spare key," he answered, as though it were obvious.

The key. Of course. The key was her reason for being in his apartment. She made herself think even as her eyes continued roaming his apartment. "Julia has a copy, but she and Phil aren't home, and they sometimes stay out until the bars close."

"That could be another couple hours," Riley remarked.

When he grew silent, she strained her ears but all she heard was the hum of his refrigerator and her own even breaths. Nobody else seemed to be in the apartment, after all.

Relief made her feel light-headed, and a harsh truth struck her. She hadn't barged into Riley's apartment in the hopes of proving Lana was with him.

She'd wanted, more than anything, to prove that she wasn't.

She turned to face him. The lateness of the hour added an intimacy to the apartment that wasn't present in the daylight. Shadows played over his face, emphasizing his lean cheeks and making his dark eyes unreadable.

She should confess that she had her key and leave, but she couldn't make herself do it, not when the air between them seemed charged with promise.

"Can I stay here until Julia gets home?" she whispered.

"You could," he answered slowly, and she waited for him to give in to the inevitable and reach for her. "But I have a better idea."

He disappeared into the kitchen. Confused, she trailed him and watched him rummage through a drawer beside the stove. After a moment, he pulled out a screwdriver.

"What's that for?" she asked.

"I'm pretty sure I can break in through your kitchen window," he said and headed for the balcony.

That's when it struck her that she'd been able to see into every room in his apartment except the bedroom, which was obviously where he had the other woman stashed.

Calling herself a fool, she blinked rapidly so the tears she felt behind her eyes wouldn't get a chance to form. Then she followed him onto the balcony.

A COOL BREEZE FROM THE harbor rustled Riley's hair and whipped through his clothes as he stood in front of Kate's kitchen window, the sill of which was no higher than his chest.

It would probably be easier to get into her apartment through the French doors, but he was fairly certain he'd break glass if he tried to jimmy the locks.

Trying to concentrate on the task and not the woman who was with him, he wedged the screwdriver between the window frame and the exterior frame.

"Riley." The voice of temptation—Kate's voice—drifted from behind him. "There's something I have to tell you."

He'd listen to what it was later, after he got the window open—when there was no chance of him suggesting she while away the time in his bed waiting for her spare key to arrive.

He jerked the screwdriver back and forth, and the window popped free of the exterior frame. A large, jagged crack instantly formed down the center of the glass pane.

"Oh, hell," he said on a groan, then slanted her a guilty look. "I'll pay for the damage, of course."

She crossed her arms over her chest but he couldn't read her expression in the darkness.

"What were you going to say?" he asked.

She shook her head. "It's not important anymore."

He might have pressed her for more of an answer if his feet weren't freezing. In a hurry to finish the job, he reached through the crack between the window and the frame into Kate's kitchen. When he located the handle, he cranked it until the opening was large enough to crawl through.

"Making progress," he told Kate, a declaration which met with silence.

He hoisted himself up, banged his knee on the sill and his elbow on the faucet before swinging his legs inside the apartment. He scooted forward, and his rear end landed hard on her kitchen counter.

Resigned to being sore in the morning, he hopped down to the floor and switched on the apartment's interior lights. Moments later, he opened the French doors to let her inside.

"Thanks," she said shortly, brushing by him. "You can go now."

He frowned. "I really am sorry about the window."

"I'm sure you are, but next time..." Her voice trailed off. "Oh, never mind."

Sensing she'd been about to say something important, he circled around to stand in front of her. "No," he said. "Tell me what's on your mind."

He could see her carrying on an internal struggle before she said, "It's nothing. Really. But next time something like this happens, you can be honest with me. Tell me to get lost, to go knock on another neighbor's door."

"You think I was trying to get rid of you?" he asked, grabbing her lightly by the shoulders when it seemed she might move away from him.

"Weren't you?"

Even though he touched only her shoulders, lust raced through his blood and he had to refrain from crushing his mouth to hers. She was right, he silently admitted. He had been trying to get rid of her.

Back there in his apartment, when the intimacy of the night had wrapped around them like a web of spun silk, he hadn't trusted himself to be alone with her. Not without making the same mistake all over again.

Slow and steady, he reminded himself. The words conjured up a ridiculous image from childhood of the tortoise who'd raced the hare and won. The tortoise plodded along, one unhurried step after another, never losing sight of the finish line.

But the tortoise hadn't faced temptation anywhere near as strong as this along the way.

When he didn't answer, she lifted both her arms, knocking his hands off her shoulders.

"Just leave, Riley."

She turned her back and moved deeper into her living room, removing her jacket with jerky motions as she went. Something fell out of her pocket and clattered to the wood floor.

Riley automatically bent down, but Kate snatched up the shiny, silver item first. She shoved it deep into the pocket of her purple miniskirt, but not before he got a good look at it.

Not understanding, he gazed up at her from where he still crouched. "That was your key."

Her throat muscles constricted when she swallowed, and her eyes shifted. "I, um, must not have checked my jacket pocket," she said after a long pause.

He didn't believe her. Not when she'd scooped up the key and tried to hide it. He straightened and met her eyes.

"What's going on, Katie?"

9

KATE FOUGHT TO KEEP from covering her face with her hands. How had she made such a stupid mistake?

"Katie?" he pressed.

He used to call her by that nickname last year, when they'd been in bed together. She considered it a low blow, especially because she wasn't the woman in his bed right now. Her voice wanted to tremble, but she wouldn't let it.

"Okay. I admit it. I wasn't locked out of my apartment."

"I gathered that much." An indentation formed between his eyebrows. "Want to tell me why you said you were?"

"Not particularly," she answered, then sighed. "But I will. I wanted to see if Lana was with you."

His eyes widened and his mouth parted, both signs of surprise. But why should it come as a shock to him that she'd guessed correctly?

Come to think of it, why had he gone to such lengths to make sure she didn't know the other woman was in his apartment? Was it because he thought his chances of getting Kate in his bed would decrease if she knew he was also sharing it with someone else?

Her chin, which had felt suspiciously quivery when they'd begun the conversation, firmed up. How dare he!

"Look, I know I shouldn't have lied to you," she said. "It was a rotten thing to do, okay? But it's not like you were upfront with me."

"What wasn't I upfront about?"

"The reason you should be getting back to your apartment instead of standing here talking to me. I know Lana's in there, Riley."

"What?"

It irked her that he still wouldn't come clean. Didn't he realize his insistence on breaking into her apartment—barefoot, no less—had tipped his hand? She might not know him well, but she did know he wasn't impatient.

"I know what you said about the two of you being friends. But when we went to the ladies' room, Lana said she was going to change that."

"So you made the flying leap that I broke into your apartment so you wouldn't discover I had Lana stowed away in my bedroom?" he asked, his voice rising.

"Yes," Kate shouted back at him. A muscle worked in his jaw and his eyes glittered, and for the first time that evening she considered that she might have jumped to the wrong conclusion. In a much quieter voice, she asked, "Don't you?"

"No, I don't." He shook his head. "Okay, yes,

Lana made it clear she wanted me. But it takes more than what one person wants for something to happen."

"So you didn't sleep with her?"

"No, I didn't sleep with her. I have no intention of sleeping with her."

Relief made her legs go weak and her eyes turn watery. Because he watched her closely for a reaction, she locked her knees and blinked to dry up the moisture.

Too late, she realized the magnitude of her mistake. She'd been trying to get him to admit he was angling for more than friendship. Not to let him guess that, after all this time, she still wanted more from him than he could give.

"Forget that I asked." She shook her head. "It's none of my business."

He reached for a strand of her hair, slid it between his fingers, then tucked it behind her ear. "What if I'd like to make it your business?"

Her heart gave a leap worthy of an Olympic hurdler. She told herself to make like one and run, but she couldn't seem to move. The only muscle getting any exercise was her heart, which raced.

"I don't know what you mean," she said, although she did. God help her, she did.

He took her right hand in his larger one and placed it over his heart. His eyes locked on hers. Even though it was winter, the air felt as thick as it did on any sultry, summer day.

"It's still there between us, Katie," he whispered. "Can't you feel it?"

"Yes," she said, the word so soft she barely heard herself say it. She meant to add that she didn't want to feel whatever still simmered between them. But she couldn't speak at all when he lifted her hand and placed a kiss in the center of her palm.

"I don't want to rush you, but I do want to kiss you." He held on to both her hand and her gaze. "Can I kiss you?"

She knew what her answer should be, but her lips wouldn't form it. From the moment they'd met, the air around them had been charged with an unseen force that drew them together. The force hadn't lessened.

She cleared her throat, moistened lips that had suddenly gone dry and let him see her need.

"You'd better," she said, and this time her words were strong and clear.

His smile looked sexy and a little bit dangerous. He tugged on her hand, drawing her toward him. She tilted her head back, and he brought his mouth down and pressed kisses the length of her mouth.

Even though his lips were soft, she felt the connection like a powerful current that surged from her head to her toes. He must have felt the charge, too, because the kiss changed almost immediately, his lips turning harder, hotter, more demanding.

She slid her hands over the hard plane of his chest, traced his broad shoulders, then looped them around her neck where she could bury her fingers in the short hairs at his nape.

One of his hands glided over her hip and anchored at the small of her back, pulling her closer. She went willingly, pressing against him from knee to chest as her nerve endings danced and heat pooled in her core.

She had her eyes closed, but she could have been blind and known it was Riley who held her. He not only smelled like no other man—a unique blend of clean soap and musky male—but also touched her exactly the way she hungered to be touched.

His hands roamed; stroking, caressing, exciting.

He deepened the kiss, his tongue licking inside her mouth as it advanced and retreated. Her heart beat hard and fast, and she heard somebody moan, surprised to realize it was her.

Heat spread low in her belly and throbbed, deep and unrelenting. She caught his tongue, holding her lips around it and sucking. This time the moan came from Riley.

He took control of the kiss, angling his head so he could kiss her more thoroughly. He pulled her harder against him, and she felt his erection. She rubbed sensuously against him and drew one of his questing hands to her breast.

He caressed her through her clothes, making her nipple pebble, creating tugs of lust in her feminine core. He kissed her deeply, wetly. Sensations, buried but never forgotten, rose up and engulfed her.

She wanted to rip off his clothes, strip off her own and erase the last year so that they were back at the place where they'd been happiest. In bed. Losing themselves in each other.

She wanted it with a desperation that bordered on

pain. But then she'd be putting herself in that vulnerable position where nothing in her life was more important than Riley.

Panic, more powerful than the passion, raced through her when she realized she was almost there now.

She couldn't bring herself to wrench out of his arms, but managed to turn her mouth. "Riley, stop," she rasped.

"Stop?" His hand still rested on her breast. His eyes, glazed with lust, looked confused. And why shouldn't they, when all the parts of her body except her mouth had given him the all-systems-go sign?

"Stop," she repeated, hating herself for not underlining the word by wrenching out of his arms. But she couldn't manage to move.

He bit his lower lip and closed his eyes, his battle with self-control evident in the whitening around his mouth. After a long moment, he dropped his hands and stepped back.

Cool air seemed to whoosh over her. She wrapped her arms around her midsection, feeling bereft. "You stopped."

"You asked me to," he said, his voice still low and husky.

He was right. She had asked him to stop. But she realized with a sinking heart that she hadn't wanted stopping to be easier for him than it had been for her.

"I figure this proves you lied about wanting to be friends," she said.

He dragged a hand through his hair, looking so

miserable that she felt no satisfaction over calling his bluff and winning.

"That wasn't a lie. I do want to be your friend."

"But you want sex, too?"

"I can't be around you without wanting to make love to you," he said in a low, urgent voice.

She rubbed a hand over her mouth, miserably aware that he was only with her because of circumstance and convenience. If the last vacant sublet in Charleston hadn't been next door, he wouldn't have given her a second thought.

"You need to go," she said.

His chest expanded, then contracted. His hair was mussed from her fingers, his shirt loosened from the waistband of his pants. Merely looking at him started a throbbing low in her body. All over again.

Before he let himself out, he stood in the moonlight streaming through the French doors and said, "I'll settle for friendship if that's all you're willing to give. It's up to you."

She stood in the same spot for a long time after he left. It was up to her, he'd said. As though it didn't matter a hell of a lot to him either way.

She shut her eyes tight but tears still seeped from them. She knew from experience that Riley couldn't give her what she needed, so how had she found herself falling for him all over again?

DAVE'S BOOTS KICKED UP dirt as he strode across the construction site toward Riley, who had arrived a whole minute and a half ago.

Preparing himself to get blasted with news of the latest trouble on site, Riley waited his brother out. But what was this? Beneath the hard hat, Dave's face wasn't grim. And was he actually smiling?

"Good news, little brother." Yes. That was a smile. A big, wide one. "We got the restaurant job."

"Well, hot damn," Riley said, enjoying a burst of pleasure. "I didn't think they'd decide so quick."

"What's to decide? We're the best. We should change the name of the business to Studs R Us."

Riley laughed. "Then we'd sound like we were running an escort service."

"When you're hot, you're hot," Dave said. "I wouldn't mind doing a little escorting on the side if we weren't going to be so busy."

"How busy are we going to be?"

"The Lowcountry Group is talking of starting construction about the time we finish up the hotel."

"We can do that," Riley said, already working on figuring out how to free up more of his time for design.

"You're supposed to give Bob Stein a call," Dave said, referring to the president and main decision-maker of the group. "He wants you sitting in on the meetings when they interview interior designers."

"They're not going with the same firm they used on this hotel?"

"Nope. Interior Treasures' fees have reportedly skyrocketed. Bob says they're looking to hire a newer, less expensive firm."

"That'll be quite the opportunity for somebody,"

Riley said. *Opportunity.* The word snagged in his brain. Kate was an interior designer. Not only that, she'd expressed a desire to work on commercial projects.

Sometimes, he thought, opportunity could work two ways.

"Do you think they'd take a recommendation?" he asked Dave, trying to sound casual.

"Sure. Why not? They'd probably be glad for it. Oh, hell."

"Excuse me?"

"Oh, hell." Dave repeated with an expression as steely as the scaffolding. "Your ex is an interior designer. That's who you're thinking of recommending."

Riley moved his shoulders up, then down. "So what?"

"So, what's going on? Are you two back together? Is that why you want to throw work her way?"

"No, we're not back together. We're friends," Riley said tightly, although he wasn't sure if that were true anymore. Friends interacted. Since he'd kissed her, Kate had become an expert on avoiding him. "And Kate doesn't need work thrown at her. She's very talented."

"So you thought of her because of her talent? Not because you're tired of this friends crap and want to sleep with her?"

That, too, Riley thought. But at this point, he'd settle for a conversation of more than a half dozen words.

He'd thought about forcing the issue last night, but Kate had been out on another date with yet another man. He'd seen them leave, and his insides had twisted like the paths of a maze.

"What I want is for Kate to get the job," Riley said.

"You also want her to be grateful enough for the recommendation that she sleeps with you. Makes perfect sense to me."

Riley shook his head. "With an attitude like that, it's a wonder you ever get laid."

"But I do, little brother," Dave said with an uplifted eyebrow, "which, I'm thinking, is more than you can say."

KATE STROVE TO KEEP her knees from knocking and her voice from shaking as four pairs of male eyes assessed her as she finished her presentation.

"The restaurant is far enough from the Historic District that we can do something a little different with the decor. The Tuscan style is popular now. Or maybe we'll want to go high tech—stainless steel, metal tubing, chrome and black accents. Whatever the decision, I'm the designer who can pull it off."

Four male heads, including Riley's, nodded. But Riley was the only one of the four men deciding her professional fate who winked at her.

The other three formed the brain trust of the Lowcountry Group, which was vigorously pursuing a share of Charleston's tourist dollars by building hotels and restaurants throughout the area.

Bob Stein, the president of the group, over-shadowed the other two. With a full head of dark hair and a florid face that hinted at a love of food and drink, he seemed formidable. But Riley had briefed Kate beforehand that he was more bark than bite.

"Thank you, Ms. Marino. That was quite impressive. We have a few other designers to interview but we'll get back to you with a decision by Monday," Mr. Stein said.

"Thank you for the opportunity," Kate said, then decided to address what the men might perceive as her weakness. "What I lack in experience, I'll make up for in enthusiasm and hard work. You won't regret it if you choose me."

"I don't believe we would," Mr. Stein said.

Kate nodded at the men, gathered her materials and stuffed them in her crimson portfolio case. She felt Riley beside her before she saw him. He looked wonderfully windblown, with his khakis and dress shirt slightly wrinkled, as though he'd come from the job site.

"I'll walk you to the elevator," Riley offered.

She waited until they'd cleared the meeting room before she asked, "How do you think I did?"

"I think you were fantastic."

"If you're only saying that because you want to sleep with me, I may have to coldcock you."

He let out a shout of laughter. The sound, rich and low, warmed her like a fire on a wintry day.

"That's not the only reason I'm saying it. I really

did think you were outstanding. Professional. Confident. And did I mention sexy as hell?"

She cut her eyes at him. "You're flirting with me."

"Is that allowed?"

"Are you kidding? After you got me this interview, you have carte blanche."

He'd phoned her three days ago to ask if she'd be interested in designing the interior of a new, multi-level waterfront restaurant on Daniel Island.

"Are you joking?" she'd asked.

When he'd assured her he wasn't, she'd screamed. Screamed. Right there in the middle of the living room of the vacation home she was redecorating on the Isle of Palms.

She was lucky the man who'd been delivering the marble statue of a nude Venus hadn't dropped it.

"In that case," he said, leaning down so that his mouth was close to her ear, "want to finish what we started the other night?"

They'd reached the elevator, which was around a corner from the hallway and relatively isolated. She deliberately pressed the down button before gazing up at him through her lashes. "It depends. How much say do you have in who gets the job?"

His eyes smiled down at her. "You're an interior designer. You should know that the architect and the interior designer work *very closely* together."

She took a step toward him and walked her fingers up his chest. This, she thought, was fun. Especially since she'd begun to suspect she just might be wrong about how he felt about her.

"In that case," she said in her huskiest voice, "I'll take a rain check. Wouldn't want you to get accused of a sex-for-hire scheme."

His face fell, his disappointment so obvious that a thrill coursed down the length of her body. Even though she was still on a high from the interview, she easily recognized the buzz as sexual.

"But I'm not the one doing the hiring," he protested.

She traced his bottom lip with the pad of her forefinger, feeling like a vixen when his eyes darkened and his breathing changed. "An even better reason to take a rain check."

He closed his eyes. Amusement mingled with desire when he opened them. "Now *you're* flirting with *me.*"

"Is that okay?" she asked, feigning wide-eyed innocence.

"Oh, yeah. In fact, you can flirt with me tonight if you like. Say, about eight? At my place?"

She laughed. "I'm heading to Savannah right now to check out some new merchandise at a couple stores I like. I'm spending the night with a girlfriend."

"When you come back," he said, "you should be prepared for me to take you up on that rain check."

She concentrated on making her brows dance so the rest of her wouldn't shiver in sexual anticipation. A tone signaled the arrival of the elevator. She waited a beat, dropped her hand and backed inside the car.

"Promises, promises," she said lightly before

lowering her voice a full octave. "Let's hope you keep them."

The door slid closed on his stunned face. She giggled to herself and swung around three hundred sixty degrees. It might have been a mistake to let him know she wanted to get involved again, but she didn't think so.

Days after she'd mentioned her desire to work on commercial projects, he'd seen to it that she had this fabulous opportunity to fulfill her career dreams. He'd even left her alone for the past few days so she could work up a presentation. Didn't that mean he cared about her?

She still hadn't come down from her high when the elevator reached the bottom floor. Humming to herself and swinging her portfolio case in a happy arc, she stepped into the lobby, got three steps and stopped.

"My, oh my," drawled Elle Dumont. "If it isn't the competition."

Elle, as usual, looked fantastic. Her blond hair was expertly colored, her designer suit a vibrant shade of Christmassy red and her smile so pretty, it would have been hard for a passerby to tell it was insincere. Kate's eyes dipped to the black leather portfolio case she carried.

"Are you here to interview for the restaurant job?" Kate asked, even though her sinking stomach proved she already knew the answer.

Elle made a tsking sound. "You didn't think you were the only one, did you?"

Kate refused to let the other woman's mock-playful tone bait her. "On the contrary, I know there's competition for any job of this magnitude."

"Of course you do, honey. But I do get the feeling that Riley didn't tell you the competition would be me," Elle said with a shake of her golden hair. "Now, if you'll excuse me, I don't want to keep the gentlemen upstairs waiting. Wish me luck."

"I'd rather not."

Elle laughed, tossing over her shoulder as she resumed her path to the elevator, "That's okay. With my connections, I don't need luck."

Kate made her feet move in the opposite direction, determined not to give Elle the satisfaction of knowing her blows had connected.

A moment ago, she'd been so sure that Riley recommending her to the Lowcountry Group meant he cared about her. But had he also recommended Elle?

10

SOMETIMES, LIVING RIGHT paid off, Riley thought as he pulled his SUV behind Kate's electric-green Toyota.

He hadn't attended Sunday services this morning to pray for Kate's return, but he couldn't deny that he wanted her back. And here she was, a day later than he'd expected but worth the wait.

Good thing he'd gone the safe route and picked up tickets for tonight instead of yesterday. When a man had bad news to break, tickets couldn't hurt.

He wanted to rush out of his car and over to her side the instant he turned off the ignition, but forced himself to take his time.

Slow and steady, he reminded himself, as he unhurriedly opened his car door and joined her on the sidewalk.

A cool December breeze blew through her hair as she swung an overnight bag from the passenger seat. She wore high, black boots with stiletto heels and yet another winter coat. This one had a black-and-white print that would have caused most women to look ridiculous. With the heightened color in her cheeks from the cold, combined with her usual inner glow, she looked stunning.

"Hey, Kate," he said as he approached. "How was the trip?"

She glanced at him before banging the door shut. "Okay."

"Let me get that bag for you," he offered.

"No need." She started up the sidewalk to the house, the bag slung over her shoulder bouncing against her back.

After a beat, he fell in step beside her. He hadn't seen her in almost forty-eight hours, not since she'd gotten him hot and bothered at the elevator.

She didn't seem to have any interest in getting him hot and bothered now.

"I expected you back yesterday. You sure the trip went okay?" He tried to read her expression, which was difficult considering he only had a view of her profile. "You want to talk about anything, I'm here."

"It went fine. I decided to stay an extra day, is all," she said before climbing the porch steps and going into the house.

When she stopped to check her mail slot, he decided to play his trump card.

"Remember how we missed out on the progressive dinner through the Historic District last year because it was a sellout? I lucked out and got a couple of tickets for tonight."

She didn't reply, and he tried not to get discouraged by the lack of enthusiasm in her expression.

"It doesn't start until five-thirty, so you'd have a

couple hours to rest up from your trip," he continued.

"I can't go."

The hairs standing up on the back of his neck alerted him that something had changed since he'd seen her at the elevator. But what?

And suddenly he knew. He didn't have to break the bad news to her. She was already aware of it.

"You ran into Elle after your interview Friday, didn't you?" he asked.

The quick flash of heat in her eyes told him he'd hit the mark. He'd thought Elle's appointment had been scheduled late enough after Kate's that their paths wouldn't cross. But, knowing Elle, she'd probably arrived early so she could spend time primping in the rest room.

"I didn't know Elle was up for the job myself until Friday." He leveled her with a stare. "Someone from the Lowcountry Group asked her to do a presentation, not me."

Her shrug looked affected. "It's no big deal. I expected to have competition."

"But you didn't expect the competition to be Elle."

"It doesn't matter who the competition is. One designer is the same as the next."

She didn't believe that any more than he did. If it weren't for Elle Dumont, he and Kate might still be together. He took a step toward her and felt the sizzle, the same as he always did. But the sizzle wouldn't survive if he couldn't get her to believe him.

"Elle doesn't mean anything to me, Kate," he said in a low, urgent voice. "She never did."

Doubt flashed in her eyes but she merely shrugged. "Water under the bridge, Riley."

But was it? Or was the water rising, threatening to sink their second chance?

She turned, breaking the invisible connection that had made the air seem thick. She bent to pick up the bag she'd put down when she checked her mail.

"Sure I can't carry that for you?" he asked.

"I'm sure," she said and rounded the corner to the stairway. He was right behind her, but it felt as though Elle was between them.

He raised his eyes to the ceiling. This was ridiculous. He couldn't let the other woman get between them. Not again. Not when Kate was the woman who mattered, and always had.

"You sure you won't change your mind about the progressive dinner?" he asked when they reached her door. He continued in his best imitation of a tour guide. "Hors d'oeuvres and eggnog at King's Courtyard Inn, followed by a carriage ride to the Wentworth Mansion for salad and entrees and on to the John Rutledge House for dessert. It'll be one tasty evening."

"I already told you." Her voice sounded cold. "I can't."

"Can't?" he asked. "Or won't?"

"Can't," she said before opening her door and slipping inside her apartment. "I already have a date for tonight."

A date? After what happened between them Friday? When he'd been so sure that he'd been making progress on the I-want-to-be-your-lover front? At the thought of her with someone else, he felt sick to his stomach.

"With Tony Quaglio?" he asked, no longer feeling inclined to be noble and give the other man an endorsement. Riley didn't want Tony to have Kate. He wanted her for himself.

She shook her head. "No. With someone else."

Where did she find all these men? He'd only been out a handful of times since they'd broken up. Aside from their double date the other night, he hadn't dated in the last three or four months at all.

"Goodbye, Riley."

She shut the door. Even though it didn't touch him, he felt the blow as though the door had slammed into him.

A date, she'd said.

He wondered if she'd made the date before or after she discovered that Elle Dumont was her competition, but bet it was the latter.

Maybe he shouldn't have been so ready to let the subject of Elle drop. No matter what Kate claimed, he could tell that long-ago kiss still bothered her.

But would it make any difference if he explained that the torrid pace of their relationship had spooked him? And that the only reason he'd kissed Elle back was to make sure his feelings for Kate were the real thing?

He stood in the hall, puzzling over what his next step in the plan to win her back should be.

His heart told him to pound on the door, declare that she was the only woman who'd ever mattered and sweep her into his arms. But he couldn't do that.

It was too fast, too furious.

He needed a way to remind her of how good things had been between them, something to make her realize how good they could be again.

After a moment, the perfect prop occurred to him.

Whistling a jazzy Christmas tune, he left the house to get it.

"LET ME MAKE SURE I'VE got this right." Julia tucked her left leg under her body before lowering herself onto her sofa. "You came to my apartment at midnight on a Sunday night to ask if I know anyone else I could set you up with?"

Stated that way, it sounded a little crazy. Or a lot desperate. Kate didn't intend to admit to either.

"Really, Julia, you are so dramatic." Kate unbuttoned her black-and-white coat and flung it over the back of a chair. "It's only eleven forty-five."

"It's still late," Julia said. "Phil is already in bed."

"I know you never go to sleep before midnight," Kate said. "Besides, I could hardly have gotten here sooner. I was on a date."

Julia gave her the long-suffering look of an old friend even though, in actuality, they'd only known each other a few months. "What was wrong with this one?"

Kate twisted her mouth, trying to think of something. Trent Laughlin, the son of a friend of a co-worker's sister-in-law, had been perfectly nice.

She'd had trouble herself figuring out why he didn't do it for her, but Julia was waiting for an answer.

"He was boring," Kate said. "All he wanted to talk about was interior design."

"How does being interested in what you do for a living make a man boring? Seems to me that would make him a good conversationalist."

"Really, Julia, after living the job all day, I don't want to talk about it all night."

"Do you know how crazy you sound?"

Kate plopped down on the sofa beside Julia. "I think I resent that."

"If we're going to continue to be friends, I need to tell it like it is—and you're acting nuts."

"Because I'm trying to find the perfect man?"

"Because you refuse to see that he lives next door."

"Oh, no, he doesn't." Kate felt the panic rise inside her like the Charleston Harbor at high tide. "Riley might seem perfect to you but that's only because you don't know what I know."

Julia crossed her arms over her chest and leaned her head back against the sofa. She wore fuzzy pink pajamas, and her eyes looked sleepy. "Then tell me."

Kate leaped to her feet and paced from one end of the room to the other, wondering where to start.

"You know that presentation I gave Friday for the restaurant job?"

"The one the supposedly imperfect Riley Carter set up?" Julia asked rhetorically. "Yeah, I know it."

"Elle Dumont, superbitch extraordinaire, is also up for the job. She and Riley went out in high school."

"I'm getting the feeling you're jealous of this woman."

"You should see her, Julia. She's gorgeous. Tall, blond, willowy and talented to boot. And did I mention she was Riley's high school girlfriend?"

"Twice. But high school was, what, like ten years ago?"

"But she's still in his life. She's even the reason we broke up. Last December I went to a restaurant to meet Riley for dinner." Kate paused, because remembering still hurt. "I saw him and Elle at the table. Kissing."

"Back up. You're saying Riley arranged to meet you and then let you catch him with another woman?"

"No," Kate said slowly. "Elle was working for the same design firm as I was back then. She relayed the message about where and when I should meet him."

"There you have it," Julia said smugly. "She set it up so you'd walk in on them."

"I know that," Kate said. And she did. She always had. "But you didn't listen. I saw them kissing."

"Did you see them having sex?"

"They were in a restaurant. Of course I didn't see them having sex."

"Let me put it another way. Do you think Riley

was having an affair with the superbitch while he was dating you?"

Despite the painful subject, a corner of Kate's mouth lifted at the way Julia had embraced her description of Elle.

Kate thought back to last year's steamy December. She and Riley had spent so many nights in bed together, he wouldn't have had the time or energy to be with anyone else.

"No," she said slowly, "I don't."

"Then I don't get what the big deal is."

"The big deal is that Elle is still in his life. Didn't you hear me? She's up for the restaurant job. You should have seen how obnoxious she was when I ran into her. She figured out Riley hadn't told me she was in the running and took delight in taunting me about it."

"Is Riley the one who asked her to submit a proposal?"

"He says he didn't know anything about it until she walked into the interview," Kate said.

"Do you believe him?"

Kate let herself think about that. She'd been so thrown by Elle's sudden emergence as a competitor that she hadn't considered whether she believed his explanation or not.

"Yeah, I do believe him," she admitted.

"Next question. Do you think Riley is involved with the superbitch right now?"

Kate didn't have to think as hard about this answer. "No, I don't."

"Okay, let's review," Julia said like the school-teacher she was. "Last year Riley's ex-girlfriend tried to get you to believe something was going on between them. This year, she's still at it. Right?"

"Right."

"But logically you know it's not true."

"Right," Kate said in a smaller voice.

"So I repeat, I fail to see the problem."

"The problem is that he kissed her back," Kate snapped.

"So what? You said the superbitch is beautiful. She kissed him. He kissed her back. It didn't have to mean anything."

"But I was so in love with him last year that I couldn't even look at another man," Kate blurted out.

"Aah," Julia said. "Now we're getting somewhere."

Kate ran the fingers of her right hand through her already tousled hair. "Care to explain that comment?"

"Suppose you tell me why it's so terrible to be head over heels about someone?"

"You wouldn't ask that if you knew my mother. All loving my dad has ever gotten her was grief."

"So he cheats on her?"

Kate frowned. In all the years her parents had been married, she'd never gotten a hint that Dad was stepping out. "I don't think he does cheat on her, but that doesn't mean anything."

"It could mean he loves her," Julia said, then narrowed her eyes and peered at Kate. "You do think your dad loves your mom, don't you?"

Kate thought about the question for a moment. "If he loves her, he doesn't love her nearly enough. If he did, he wouldn't gamble and lose jobs and lie to her."

"Ah," Julia said, drawing out the syllable, "I understand now."

"What do you mean? What do you understand?"

"Your problem with Riley."

Kate glowered at her, because the conclusion she'd reached was only too clear. "You think I'm afraid I'm going to end up like my mother."

"Aren't you?"

Kate swallowed, trying to bank the fear rising up to choke her. Deep down, she'd always known her problem with Riley didn't have anything to do with Elle. But she hadn't considered that it had something to do with her mother.

"So what if I am afraid?" she finally asked. "Riley's never told me he loves me. What's wrong with protecting myself from getting hurt?"

"Nothing," Julia said, and Kate breathed a little easier. But only for a moment. "That is, if you're right about how he feels about you. But what if you're wrong? What if he loves you back?"

RILEY SAT, EXHAUSTED in the glow of the seven-foot Douglas fir he'd picked up at a roadside stand and spent the day failing to make beautiful.

The decorations weren't the problem. Kate had

picked them out last year after she'd talked him into putting up a Christmas tree at his beach house. She had impeccable taste, even if she did favor oddly shaped ornaments in the unusual Christmas color combination of pink and purple.

The problem was that a tree was just a tree if you had no one to share it with.

His plan had been to use the tree to remind Kate of their last Christmas together. But it was after midnight and she'd yet to return to her apartment.

She was in the building, though. He'd seen her return thirty minutes ago with some guy wearing so much product, the wind hadn't been able to budge his hair.

She must have sent the guy packing at the foyer to the house, because he'd heard only one set of footsteps coming up the stairs when he'd cracked open his door. The footsteps had continued to the third level, causing him to conclude that Kate was upstairs talking to Julia.

That was probably just as well. Appearing at Kate's door in the wee hours to tell her he had something to show her wasn't the act of a patient man.

The tortoise popped out of its shell and into his mind. Slow and steady, it said.

Other images quickly replaced the talking turtle. Of Kate walking her fingers up his chest as she'd looked at him from under her lashes. Of the promise in her eyes when she'd flirted with him. Of the passion that had always bubbled between them, making it so very hard to think.

The passion rose in him like a live thing, urging him to go upstairs to Julia's apartment and act on what he felt sure they both wanted.

Slow and steady, the tortoise warned again.

"Forget that, turtle," Riley said aloud. "You ever hear the one about the boat sailing if you wait too long?"

Before he could remind himself that careful and patient were what had always worked best for him, he jumped to his feet. Julia liked him. She'd understand if he pounded on her door, barged into the apartment and did whatever he could think of to get Kate to leave with him.

He flung open his own door, stepped into the hall and froze. Kate wasn't with Julia. She was right here, in front of the open door of her apartment.

With her artfully untidy hair and the winter-white jeans she'd paired with a lavender turtleneck, she looked like a fashion plate. But he couldn't help likening her to Alice, about to disappear into the rabbit's hole.

"Kate." He breathed her name, trying to think of something, anything, to keep her from vanishing into her apartment. "I've been waiting for you."

"Why?" She evaded his eyes, which was unlike her, but he didn't let that stop him.

"To tell you I hoped your date was lousy."

"Gee, thanks," she said with a touch of the spirit he expected from her.

Without taking his eyes from her, he pulled her apartment door closed.

"There's another reason I was waiting for you," he said in a voice that had gone low and husky. He took a breath and smelled the spicy scented lotion she liked to wear. "Want to know what it is?"

He saw a pulse beat fast and furious in her neck. Her chest rose and fell, and he could hear her uneven breaths. "Why?"

"Because I want to collect on that rain check," he said, and pulled her into his apartment.

11

KATE LET RILEY DRAW HER into his apartment, her heart beating so hard it felt as if it had leaped into her throat.

What if you're wrong about how he feels about you? Julia had asked.

What if she was?

A man didn't wait up until after midnight for a woman he didn't care about. He didn't look into the eyes of that woman like he'd die if he didn't kiss her, and practically drag her into his home.

Except Riley didn't kiss her.

Without letting go of her hand, he shut the door and led her deeper into his apartment. But not toward his bedroom. Toward his living room, where a live Christmas tree that must have been seven feet tall stood glittering in the darkness.

The sight of it surprised her, because last year he'd claimed the tiny artificial one his mother had given him was good enough. If Kate hadn't pressed him to put up a tree at his beach house, he would have done without.

How many nights, she wondered, had that tree been in the background when they'd made love?

The first time, she'd been standing on a footstool stringing lights on branches when she'd lost her balance. He'd hooked an arm around her from behind so she wouldn't fall, bringing her body flush against his.

Within seconds, they'd been kissing. Within moments, they'd been naked. They hadn't made it to the bedroom. Not when the sofa was closer.

"What do you think?" His question snapped her out of the past.

She'd thought he'd been about to kiss her. She'd thought he wanted to make love to her.

Heavens, she was a fool.

Moisture gathered in her eyes, but she managed to answer despite the thickening of her throat. "It's nice."

"Nice?" He repeated the word as though it were toxic. "I hoped for more of a reaction than that."

"What did you want me to do?" she asked acerbically, but ruined the effect by sniffling. "Cartwheels?"

He sighed, low and deep. He turned her shoulders so she was forced to look at him. Cupping her cheek, he trailed his fingers down, over and across her mouth. Her lips trembled.

"I wanted to make you remember," he whispered.

She blinked hard so the tears in her eyes wouldn't fall. "Remember what?"

"This," he said before he bent his head and kissed her.

Not tentatively, like a man in control of his emotions. But passionately, as though he couldn't stop himself.

She closed her eyes, trying to stem the surge of raw desire that threatened to consume her. But it was useless. She hadn't been able to fight what she felt for him a year ago, when they'd been virtual strangers. Now that she knew him better, resistance was impossible.

Because she loved him.

Even as she sank into the kiss, fear, like a ferocious ocean wave, washed over her.

She loved him. But the thought of making love to him scared her to death. Her emotions were so raw, her feelings so intense, that she wouldn't be able to disguise how much she wanted him.

And what if he didn't want her in the same way?

Before she could think about pulling away, Julia's voice echoed in her head: *What if he loves you back?*

He lifted his head, breaking off a kiss she'd wanted more than food, more than water, more than breath. She squeezed her eyes shut, willing herself not to cry. But then she felt gentle hands cup her cheeks, and she opened her eyes to see him gazing back at her.

"Just so we're clear, I put up the tree to remind you of how it used to be between us," he said in a low, earnest voice. "And to let you know I want that again."

"Then I was right all along," she said with a hitch in her voice. "You do want sex."

"You were wrong." He shook his head. "What I want is you."

She'd barely had time to process his meaning before he brought his mouth down to hers a second time. The heat flared, insistent and impossible to contain, and then she was lost.

"Ah, Katie," he rasped against her mouth. "I don't think I can go slow."

"Then don't," she said and deepened the kiss, parting his lips with her tongue. He opened to her, circling her tongue with his, letting the kiss become more urgent, more passionate.

Needing to touch more of him, she yanked his shirt from the waistband of his jeans and put her hands on his naked skin. Starting at his abdomen, she traced the lines of his pectoral muscles upward with frantic fingers.

He groaned when she reached his nipples and rubbed, and she felt his erection against her lower body. He slanted his mouth over hers, deepening the kiss even further.

Blood rushed through her, like a heated river. She slid her hands down his bare chest, then tugged at his shirt. It nearly killed her to break contact with his mouth so she could yank it over his head.

But he was all sinew and muscle, so beautiful that she could have cried. She ran her hands over the hairs of his chest, loving the feel of him, loving him.

She let the flood of familiar sensations steal over her. A year ago, the intensity of those feelings had frightened her. They still did. But there was nothing she could do to stop them.

His hands were everywhere. In her hair. At her

breasts. Cupping her rear end to bring her sex against his erection. She yielded willingly, her body sliding against his, her hands reaching for what she couldn't get enough of.

Now that he was in her arms again, she didn't want to let him go. Not now. Not ever.

His mouth moved to her neck. She arched her head back, and sensuous shivers ran down her body as he nibbled.

"I want you naked," he said, and then proceeded to get her that way, yanking the turtleneck over her head and fumbling with the front clasp of her bra.

When her breasts spilled free of the flimsy material, he filled his hands with them, making her arch her back and gasp. His mouth, hot and wet, replaced his hands, his tongue laving her nipples as something liquid and urgent pooled in her center.

His hands were at the waistband of her pants now, tugging down the zipper and then the pants, taking her skimpy panties along with them. He trailed hot, open-mouthed kisses down her abdomen as he got to his knees, shimmying the pants all the way off.

When he dipped his tongue into her navel, she moaned. When his mouth moved lower, her eyes rolled back in her head.

The feelings were so intense that she would have squirmed away from him, but he filled his hands with her buttocks, urged her legs apart with his chin and delved into her sex with his tongue.

"Riley," she gasped at the first wet thrust.

He gazed up at her, the look dark and wicked. "You don't want me to stop, do you?"

Silently she shook her head. He held her in place and she made helpless little sounds as she let him go to work. Sensations spiraled inside her at the hot, wet thrusts. She tangled her hands in his hair, wordlessly urging him on while emotion sang through her body and her legs went weak.

The orgasm hit her so hard and so quickly that her eyes went blind. She cried out at the pleasure, dimly realizing that she hadn't felt anything like it since the last time they were together.

Holding her so she wouldn't fall, he kissed his way up her body. She felt rough cotton against her naked legs and realized he still wore his jeans.

"Your turn to get naked," she said against his mouth.

"Gladly," he replied with a smile so sexy, the heat of it penetrated clear through her heart.

She'd grown accustomed to Riley taking things slowly over the past weeks, but he did her bidding with a speed that made her head spin.

Tugging at his zipper, he pushed the jeans down his hips to reveal plain white boxers. On anyone else, the boxers would have looked boring. But on Riley, who was bare-chested and aroused, they were so sexy she could barely breathe. He made short work of them, revealing an erection so impressive she thought her heart might need to be jump-started.

The lights on the tree cast him in a soft glow,

backlighting his hair and muting the lines of his perfect body.

He stared at her for a moment, saying nothing, then hooked an arm under her knees and lifted her. She felt boneless when he picked her up and laid her down on the sofa. But she couldn't give in to the wonderful lethargy, not when there was something she wanted to do for him.

Before he could join her on the sofa, she sat up and stopped him. "Your turn," she said and took him into her mouth.

She closed her lips over him, swirling her tongue over the head of his penis, delighting in the way he moaned. She slid her mouth up and down, feeling his leg muscles tense, feeling female and powerful.

"Katie, stop," he said in a shaky voice after a few moments. "I want to come inside you."

She wanted that, too. So she took her mouth from him and gazed up at him, trusting him completely, loving him more.

"Condom?" she asked.

He shut his eyes, and for one terrible moment she thought he might not have one. But then he held up a finger, said, "Be back in a flash," and tripped over the coffee table in his haste to get to the bedroom.

When he returned carrying a fistful of condoms, she was still smiling.

"What?" he said.

"You even look sexy falling down."

He smiled back. "Nearly falling down," he corrected, then ripped into a condom package and broke speed records putting it on.

She opened her arms, her doubts gone. This was the man she loved, the man she wanted to spend her life with.

"I'll go slow," he said, but she pulled him down and aligned her naked body with his. She lifted her hips in invitation.

"Or maybe I won't," he said tightly and drove inside her, which was fine with her. She didn't want to go slow. She wanted him to want her without thought, the same way she wanted him.

"Katie." His words were barely distinguishable as he moved inside her. "I've missed this. I've missed you."

"I've missed you, too," she said.

And then she couldn't speak, because the heat swept over her, burning out the words and leaving only feeling. How had she lived without this? How had she lived without him?

His thrusts started out slow and steady, but she lifted her hips to meet him and the rhythm changed to fast and furious.

The feelings spiraled inside her, like a tornado that had been let loose. It was exactly the kind of thing that had happened last year when they'd been together, but something was different this time.

Not the sensation, which burned as hot and bright as ever. Not the orgasm, which was powerful enough to register on the Richter scale. But the knowledge.

Because, as she crested a moment after he did and called out his name, she admitted something to herself that she hadn't been brave enough to face last year.

She not only loved him, she'd never be able to stop loving him.

"That was wonderful," he said against her neck when their breathing had slowed. Goose bumps popped up over the length of her body. "You're wonderful."

Not the words she wanted to hear, but he kept his arms around her, holding her close against his heart, giving her hope.

Please, God, she thought, *let him love me, too.*

RILEY LET THE WATER in the shower stream over him, telling himself he'd done the right thing by not waking Kate before he'd gotten out of bed.

He'd wanted to make love to her again, but he was running late and there wouldn't have been time for more than quick, furious lovemaking. The kind they'd indulged in repeatedly last night.

The sensual memories sent a torrent of heat through his body, and he turned down the shower knob to cool himself.

Last night had been amazing, but he needed to approach this second chance with Kate with a cool head. The next time he made love to her, he meant to go slowly so he didn't scare her off.

At least he hadn't told her he loved her. He'd nearly blurted it out a dozen times last night, but then he'd remembered the plan and what had always worked best for him.

If he played the slow, steady hand, he might eventually get what he wanted more than anything in this life.

And that was her.

He stepped out of the shower and patted himself dry with a fluffy, oversized towel. Because he wanted to rush out of the bathroom and over to the bed where Kate still slept, he took his time, towel drying his hair and pulling on boxers and a pair of chinos.

He deliberately took in a slow, deep breath before opening the bathroom door and entering a bedroom that was no longer dark. Weak sunlight peeked through the blinds, casting the bed in soft focus.

Kate was lying there, stretching, looking languorously satisfied, her dark hair arranged like a cloud on the pillow underneath her head. She had the sheets pulled up nearly to her neck, but he could still see the outline of her body and knew she was naked under the covers.

She smiled at him.

Ah, hell, he thought, and did exactly what he'd told himself not to do—he rushed. He went over to the bed, where he bent down and claimed her mouth with a heady thoroughness. The blood rushed from his head to more interesting parts of his body, counteracting the effects of his cool shower.

Take it slow, his brain screamed at the rest of his body before he could whip off her covers and his clothes. He lifted his head, breaking off the kiss, and smiled, which wasn't difficult considering Kate's dazed expression. She'd obviously been as carried away as he had been.

Maybe acting on impulse wasn't so terrible after all.

"Good morning," he said, stroking her soft cheek, feeling her lean into his touch like a well-satisfied cat.

"I'll say."

He smiled wide at that. "I'd love to stay but I've got a meeting at eight o'clock."

He checked the bedside clock and got a pang when he saw it was already twenty minutes before the hour. The meeting was downtown, so he'd still be on time, but he typically liked to arrive at least fifteen minutes early to get his thoughts in order.

"Ah," she said, "why do I get the feeling it's with the brain trust of the Lowcountry Group?"

"Because it is," he said but didn't elaborate. He didn't need to. They both knew he was meeting with the Lowcountry Group to help decide which interior designer would be awarded the restaurant job.

"Then you better get dressed," she said, and he reluctantly straightened from the bed.

He pulled a camel-colored, long-sleeved jersey-knit shirt from his closet and pulled it on, then took a belt from one of the wooden slats of his belt rack.

"I hate to run off like this but I'll make it up to you," he said as he threaded his belt through the loops of his pants. "I'm not sure how yet, but I will."

He felt her eyes on him as he tucked in his shirt and pulled on socks and shoes. Aware that time was running short, he intended to say goodbye and leave. Instead, he froze. She was sitting up in bed, the sheets tucked under her arms, her hair a delightful mess, her face soft and warm.

And he loved her. Not only that, he wanted to marry her. Not next year, after a long engagement and plenty of time to plan a wedding. But next week.

Ah, hell, he thought, and crossed to the bed in three steps.

"I thought you had to run," she said.

"I have to tell you something first." He sat down on the edge of the bed. *Careful,* his internal voice of reason warned. *Don't say too much.* "This last year without you was the hardest one of my life. I don't want to go through that again."

She swallowed, but didn't reply.

"This probably isn't the right time or the right place, and I promised myself I'd take things slowly, but…"

He paused before he could give in to impulse and ask her to marry him. What in the hell was he doing? He'd already lost her once by rushing. Not only that, the timetable was all wrong.

When he did ask her to marry him, it would be after much thought to the time and the setting. Wine would flow, music would play and he'd have an engagement ring in his pocket. He couldn't ask her now, not like this. Hell, he didn't even think she was ready to hear that he loved her.

But he couldn't just leave things the way they

were, either, not when he couldn't bear the thought of living without her.

"I want you to think about us living together," he finished.

She stared at him wordlessly, and his heart beat like a jackhammer. What was she thinking?

"I'd want to keep my place on Sullivan's Island, but only for the weekends. We could either both cram into your apartment or get another, bigger place here in town. Whatever you want is fine with me," he continued, making it up as he went along. It wasn't the usual way he came up with plans, but he liked the sound of it. As long as he and Kate were together, he'd like the sound of anything.

But still she said nothing. His heart beat harder, faster.

"I know I'm rushing you, and I know that I shouldn't." He gave a self-deprecating laugh. "But I want you so damn much that I can't help myself."

He waited, watching the emotions flutter over her face. He couldn't identify any of them, but none looked like happiness.

"I have the sublet until March so we don't need to decide anything until then." He held his breath, waiting for a reply. She didn't give one. He released his breath and cocked an eyebrow. "It would be nice to know what you're thinking."

He tried to ignore the weight that pressed down on his chest. *Say yes*, he silently implored.

"I need to think about it," she said, "maybe give you an answer when I get back from Philly."

His brow furrowed at the double dose of bad news. He didn't want her to need to think about it, and he didn't want her to leave, not even for a few days. "I didn't know you were going to Philadelphia for Christmas."

"I didn't think to mention it," she said.

He waited for her to ask him to come. He had a busy week ahead but he'd go with her, even if he couldn't manage to get away for more than a few days. But she was silent.

"When do you leave?" he asked.

"Thursday."

Three days from now. Three nights in which he'd try his best to convince her that she wanted to live with him.

"Then we'll have to make the most of the time we do have together this week," he said.

"Speaking of time…" she said, and he glanced at the bedside alarm clock. Ten minutes before the hour.

Hell, if he didn't hurry, he would be late.

He kissed her on the lips, quick and hard, forcing himself to move away when he wanted to linger. At the door, he paused.

"I'll see you tonight, okay?"

She waited a beat before she answered, "Okay."

He rushed out of the apartment. *So much,* he thought, *for slow and steady.*

AFTER RILEY LEFT THE apartment, Kate used the pads of her fingers to wipe tears from under her eyes.

She felt like the biggest fool in the universe.

When he'd begun that speech about the time and the place not being right, she'd thought he was about to ask her to marry him. Her heart had hammered, her palms had grown damp and it had been hard to breathe. Because she had been going to accept.

Yes, she wanted to marry him. Yes, she wanted to spend the rest of her life with him, to have his children, to call him her husband.

But then he'd asked her to live with him, and all the fears she'd managed to talk herself out of the night before had come rushing back.

She loved him, and he loved having sex with her.

Oh, he probably cared about her. Maybe he even loved her a little. But he couldn't possibly love her as deeply as she loved him. If he did, he would have asked her to marry him, not to live with him.

She forced herself to get out of bed, use the bathroom and go through the motions of getting dressed in the same turtleneck and jeans she'd worn the night before.

Riley wasn't the only one who had to work. She needed to go next door and get ready for the day so she could finish up the interiors of that house on the Isle of Palms.

Keeping busy was a necessity, not only to lessen her anxiety about whether she'd get the restaurant job, but to keep her mind off Riley.

Because no matter how much she desired him, she couldn't live with him. She wasn't even sure she could continue to see him.

The phone rang before she could leave Riley's

bedroom. She automatically reached for the receiver, but remembered at the last second that she had no right and let the answering machine pick up.

"Hello, Riley darling, this is your mother."

A mother who lived in town but whom Kate had never met.

"I hoped I'd catch you but apparently I didn't call early enough. Give me a ring tonight, won't you, darling? I'm working on the menu for Christmas dinner and want to make absolutely sure that you're not inviting anybody. I so wish you were dating somebody special. Talk to you soon."

Kate's eyes watered again, although she would have been stunned had Riley told his mother about her. Still, it hurt that the woman didn't know she existed.

THE DAY DIDN'T GET ANY brighter as it went along. The beach house turned out beautifully, but the contractor she'd hired to put in the kitchen cabinets submitted a bill far in excess of his estimate.

While she was in her office on one line sorting out that mess, Bob Stein of the Lowcountry Group called on another to let her know she hadn't gotten the restaurant job.

She barely had time to register that crushing disappointment when the phone rang again. This time it was her teenage brother, Johnny.

"Hey, Kate. I hate to ask, but could you lend me a couple hundred bucks?" His voice was quiet, as though he didn't want anyone to overhear.

Kate frowned. Johnny had borrowed money from her before, but never this much. "What for?"

"I need to get work done on my car. I can't get a job until basketball season is over, but I'll pay you back. I swear I will."

"I know you will, Johnny. I'm just wondering why you're asking me for money instead of Mom and Dad."

"Because I'm pretty sure they don't have it. I heard Mom crying last night before Dad came home, and I think it was about money. Either that, or she's tired from working so much. With Dad out of work, things have been kind of rough here."

"Okay. You got it," Kate promised and talked with her brother for a few minutes more before hanging up the phone.

She put her elbows on her desk and her head in her hands. Things must be more dire than her mother had admitted if Johnny was asking her for money. And if Mom was crying.

She didn't have any problem giving Johnny the money but it wouldn't help her mother, all of whose problems stemmed from loving the wrong man.

The wrong man.

Kate looked down at one of the message slips on her desk that she hadn't yet dealt with. It was from Riley, who she very much feared was as wrong for her as her father was for her mother.

What was she going to do about Riley?

A slip of paper at the corner of her desk caught her eye, and everything inside her went still. She picked it up, read the name and phone number of her former boss and wondered if this were an omen.

When she'd returned his phone call a few weeks before, he'd asked if she'd be in Philadelphia over the holidays. Then he'd invited her to stop by his office to talk about getting her old job back.

She'd tried to say that would be a waste of time, but he'd convinced her to take a few weeks to think it over.

At the time, she hadn't thought there was anything to think over. Moving back to Philadelphia hadn't been a serious possibility until this very minute. Because if she stayed in Charleston, she might not have the willpower to keep away from Riley. But if she left...

Without giving herself time to second-guess what she was about to do, she picked up the phone and dialed.

12

RILEY HELD UP THE CARTON of ice cream, giving his hands something to do so he wouldn't pull Kate into his arms and resume where they'd left off that morning.

"I brought your favorite kind," he said. "Chocolate raspberry torte."

She regarded him from the open door of her apartment, her eyes guarded. The trendy hair and beautiful face were the same, but she wore brown slacks and a blouse in a muted beige instead of her usual wild colors.

She'd had a major disappointment today, and he longed to take her into his arms and comfort her. But she had her arms folded over her midsection in a pose that told him that would be a mistake.

"Thoughtful," she said. "But I'm not one of those women who eats ice cream to cheer up. When I'm upset, I prefer a drink."

"I have some wine next door. Give me a minute and I'll get it," he said.

Her voice stopped him. "No need. I'm already over not getting the restaurant job, Riley."

She made the statement in a voice that held no inflection. But could she really be over it? She'd been so excited about the opportunity, so sure it could lead her down her desired career path.

He'd wanted to break the bad news to her himself but it hadn't been his place. Even though the Lowcountry Group had consulted him, ultimately its representatives made the decision on who to hire. But he had called her after the fact to commiserate.

"Sorry I didn't call back," she said, still in that flat voice, "but it was a busy day."

"You're good at what you do, Kate. You'll have other opportunities."

"I know," she said, as though the subject were closed.

Something was wrong here, Riley thought. Something beyond disappointment that she hadn't gotten the job.

"Can I come in?" he asked.

For a moment he thought she might refuse, but then she stepped back to let him inside. "I'll put the ice cream in the freezer," she said, taking it from him.

She disappeared into the kitchen, and while he waited for her to return he thought about what could be wrong. By the time she got back, he had a pretty good idea of what it could be.

"Did Bob Stein tell you that he gave the job to Elle Dumont?" he asked.

"Even if he hadn't, she would have," she said, still in that toneless voice. "She called to congratulate me for fighting the good fight. While she was at it, she gloated the good gloat."

Once a bitch, always a bitch, he thought. "She shouldn't have done that," he said.

"Like I said, it doesn't matter."

But what if it did? What if she still had the crazy idea that he was involved with Elle? He came across the room, stopping inches shy of her.

"I went to bat for you in the meeting this morning," he said. "I told them you were the best choice. But Bob decided the restaurant should have an old-country feel, and Elle's portfolio showed a preference for working on traditional projects."

"Okay." She didn't meet his eyes, and it seemed as though the long, passionate night they'd spent in bed together had never been.

"Okay? That's your entire response? Just okay?"

"What else is there to say, Riley?" Her eyes touched on his, then looked away. "I know the architect doesn't do the hiring."

"I hope you'll be okay with me and Elle working together."

"Whether I'm okay with it doesn't matter."

"Of course it matters. I'm in your life now, Kate. Didn't you hear me this morning? I want us to live together."

"Yes, I heard you."

She looked toward her bedroom, as though wanting to get back to something. The door was ajar and he had a clear view of her bed from where he stood.

Nearly full suitcases lay atop the starburst quilt. The blood inside him seemed to stop flowing.

"Are you going somewhere?" he asked.

"Philly," she answered. "I told you that this morning."

"You told me you were going to Philadelphia on Thursday. It's Monday. A little early to start packing, I'd think."

"Change of plans." She moved to the bedroom. "You don't mind if I pack while we talk, do you? My cab will be here soon so I don't have much time."

Her cab? She was leaving and hadn't even asked him to drive her to the airport.

"When did you change your flight?" he asked.

"This afternoon." She took some silky underwear from a drawer and stuffed them into a side pocket of her suitcase. "It made sense. I haven't taken any vacation in months, and I have the time because I freed up my schedule in anticipation of getting the restaurant job."

No matter that she tried to hide it, he heard the disappointment in her voice. He wanted to comfort her, but she'd yet to give him the right. She hadn't even told him if she'd live with him yet.

"When are you getting back?"

"I haven't decided." She went to another of her drawers, removed a silky nightgown he didn't recognize and dropped it into a suitcase.

He should nod, be cool, but he couldn't. "You'll think about us living together while you're gone?"

She turned to him, very slowly, and he had a premonition of doom. "I meant to talk to you about that. I've already been thinking about it. It's not what I want, Riley."

"What?"

"It's too fast," she said.

Too fast. The words hit him so hard, he felt like he'd been sucker punched. He'd known all along that he was moving too quickly, that it was dangerous to deviate from the plan, but still he'd done it.

"We don't talk to each other for eleven months, we sleep together once and suddenly we're moving in together," she continued. "It doesn't make sense."

It did make sense. It made sense because he loved her and couldn't live without her. *Tell her,* his heart screamed. But if he did, he might lose her forever. Too fast, she'd said.

"Then we'll slow down," he said. Going back to being just friends wouldn't be easy, but he could do it if it meant keeping Kate in his life.

"That won't work, either. This is hard to say." She blinked a few times as though her eyes might be tearing. "You and I don't work together, Riley."

He swallowed hard. "We worked together fine last night."

"I'm not talking about the sex. We both know that's great. It's everything else."

He tried to draw in deep, slow breaths but could only manage fast, shallow ones. "We need time together, that's all." His words sounded choppy. "Time to get to know each other, to trust each other."

Time for you to fall in love with me, he thought. That

had been the plan until he'd blown it last night by sleeping with her.

"There's something else I should tell you," she said. "My former boss in Philly has been after me for weeks to talk to him about rejoining the firm. That's one of the reasons I'm going up early."

The news hit him so hard, he sat down on the edge of her bed. "When did you decide this?"

"Today, when I didn't get the restaurant job. My old firm has a division that specializes in hospitality design and tends to work on more modern projects, which is up my alley."

He wanted to beg her not to go and then give her a reason to stay by dragging her over to the bed and making love to her until she was weak from pleasure.

But she'd told him not fifteen minutes ago that he was rushing her. He couldn't afford to rush her now. He needed to stick with the plan, and that meant letting her know he was a friend who'd give her the time and space she needed.

"You shouldn't jump into this, Kate," he said. "You need to think hard about whether it's right for you. You want to do what'll make you happy. But whatever it is, I'm behind you."

She seemed about to say something, but then a car horn sounded outside the apartment. She peeked out her window, which overlooked the street.

"That's my cab," she said, going over to the bed and shutting her suitcase with a click that sounded final.

"I'll help you carry your bags downstairs," Riley offered, even though he'd rather cut off his own hand than help her walk out of his life.

He waited while she retrieved her toiletry bag from her bathroom, took a bag full of wrapped presents from her closet and put on her red winter coat.

Outside on the wind-whipped sidewalk, after the cab driver had packed her suitcases into the trunk, she turned to him.

"Goodbye, Riley." Her voice sounded suspiciously thick, but it could have been because the wind was howling.

Stay here with me, his heart screamed.

Too fast, his brain countered. *Too furious.*

She turned toward the cab, took a step, then turned back again. Rushing over to him, she stood on tiptoes and kissed him lightly on the lips.

His control shattered, and he gathered her close. Despite his renewed resolve to take things slowly, his mouth closed over hers and he poured all the love and passion he felt into the kiss. She looked dazed when he let her go. He felt the same way.

"I love you, Katie," he whispered, not able to hold the words back no matter how hard he tried.

The cab was idling at the curb, the passenger door open, waiting for her to get in. She backed up a few steps, her eyes locked on his.

"But not enough," she said, then turned and stepped into the cab, leaving him to wonder what she'd meant.

He loved her so much, his heart hurt as he watched the cab disappear into the distance, because he wasn't at all sure she'd ever come back to him.

13

FROM THE WINDOW OF the cramped kitchen in her parents' house, Kate watched fat, feathery flakes fall from the sky and coat south Philadelphia in a layer of snow.

Maybe now that a white Christmas was in the offing, she'd be able to rid herself of the line that kept running through her head about a blue one.

She would not have a blue Christmas without Riley. She wouldn't let herself.

"Gotta love that snow," she said in a determinedly cheerful voice. "I'd rather avoid it the rest of the year but I love it at Christmas."

Her mother paused in the act of rolling out dough on a floured section of kitchen counter and smiled at her. The years had added gray to her dark hair, a slight stoop to her shoulders and visible lines around her eyes and mouth, but she was still a beautiful woman.

"You've been that way since you were little," her mother said. "You put snow at the top of every Christmas wish list you wrote to Santa."

"Who put Italian fig cookies on their list?" Kate

made a face as she ground together the figs, raisins, nuts and dates that were earmarked for filling. "I forgot how hard these things were to make."

Her mother returned to rolling out the dough, smiling to herself as she worked the rolling pin. "You know why we make them. Your father loves them."

And Mom, Kate reminded herself, loved Dad so much, she'd do anything for him. No matter how little she got in return.

"You like them, too, don't you?" her mother asked.

"Sure," Kate lied, reluctant to dampen her mother's merry mood by admitting she'd always found it difficult to choke down one of the cookies. "But you know I live for chocolate. Personally, I think chefs should find ways to make it the main entree. Like chocolate tartare. Or chocolate Cordon Bleu. Or chocolate Marsala."

Her mother set down the rolling pin and wrapped Kate in a quick, warm hug. "Have I told you yet how wonderful it is to have you home?"

"Yes. But I don't mind hearing it again."

Her mother drew back. "You'd hear it all the time if you moved back to Philadelphia. Have you decided yet whether you're going back to your old firm?"

"Not yet," Kate said, although she wasn't sure why she hesitated. She'd been prepared to accept a job offer on the spot when she'd gone into Grant's Interiors two days ago, but instead had hesitated.

She hadn't yet decided what it was she needed to

think about. As long as Riley was in Charleston, it would be safer for her heart to be elsewhere.

"Speaking of jobs, I have some good news about your father," Mom said. "I was going to wait and let him tell you, but I can't keep it in any longer. He got that sales job he interviewed for."

"Really?" Kate's brother had told her just last night that Dad had been passed over. "When did he tell you this?"

"About an hour ago." Her mother beamed at her, looking younger than her fifty years. "I told you somebody would hire him before the holidays. Sometimes all it takes is a little faith."

She squeezed Kate's arm and finished rolling out the dough before placing teaspoonfuls of filling in rows about two inches apart. Throughout the entire process, she hummed a song about Christmas being the most wonderful time of the year.

Kate clamped her mouth shut. She doubted that Johnny's information was wrong, but her mother would leap to her father's defense if Kate accused him of having lied to her.

It would be better to wait until she could get her father alone and ask him what the truth was.

Her chance didn't come until late in the evening, after her mother had gone upstairs to take a shower and Johnny was in front of the television watching a decidedly non-Christmassy thriller.

Her father slipped out the back door, and Kate shrugged into her red coat and followed him onto the porch. The outside light was so dim that she might have had problems locating him if not for the glow of his cigarette.

"Kate. You about gave me a heart attack. I thought you were your mother."

Even in the dim light, she read relief on his face. At forty-seven, Frank Marino was still a remarkably handsome man. He had thick, dark hair, strong features punctuated by a square jaw, and no excess weight on his six-foot-plus frame.

She'd once taken pleasure in the way he looked. When she was around ten, he'd had a red convertible, and she'd thought nothing was cooler than having him pick her up after school.

That was before she'd realized he was available to pick her up because he was out of a job. Again. And before she'd figured out that her mother worked extra shifts because she couldn't count on Dad to stay employed. Kate had long since understood that Mom couldn't count on Dad for much of anything.

"Mom thinks you quit smoking." She gestured to the burning cigarette.

"I know it." He bestowed upon her a smile so charming, she wondered if he practiced it in front of a mirror. "Do me a favor and don't tell her you caught me."

She moved across the porch toward him, careful to keep out of the stream of smoke. "You don't tell her a lot of things, do you, Dad?"

He gave her the clueless look he'd mastered long ago, the one her mother fell for every time. "Excuse me?"

"Mom told me this afternoon that you're employed again, but Johnny said you didn't get the job. Which is it?"

Something flickered across his face, and for an instant, Kate thought he might lie to her, too. But then he lifted his hands in a guilty gesture. "You caught me. I don't have a job just yet."

"Then why did you tell Mom you did?"

"Because I will. I have feelers out." He thumped his chest, wiggled eyebrows that were as perfect as the rest of him. "How much longer can employers pass this up?"

He patted her cheek with the hand that didn't hold his cigarette, and smiled. "Don't look so disapproving, Kate. What's so terrible about a little white lie if it brightens your mother's holiday?"

"But you lie to her all the time, Dad. You always have. About why you got fired or where you've been or what happened to the mortgage money. You even lied to her about quitting smoking."

His shoulders stiffened, as overt a sign of anger as he ever showed. A more even-tempered man, she'd never met. "What goes on between your mother and me is none of your business, Kate."

Normally Kate would have left it at that, but years of frustration bubbled over. "It's past time that somebody called you on the way you treat Mom, because she certainly won't."

He leveled her with a stare. His eyes, she'd been told, were the exact shape and color as hers. "You ever wonder why she doesn't complain?"

"Because she believes in you. She believes every last thing you tell her."

The overhanging awning on the porch provided no protection from the wind that swept the back of the house. Kate wrapped her arms around her mid-section to keep from shivering, but couldn't be sure the cold didn't come from within.

She heard him sigh. "You don't really think your mother is that gullible, do you?"

"What do you mean?"

"That she can smell the smoke on my clothes when I come inside the house. It's a game we play, Kate. She knows I'm not telling her the truth but she doesn't care. Because I'm telling her what makes her happy." .

Kate thought about the way her mother had hummed when she baked cookies that afternoon, and of the warmth that seeped into her voice whenever she talked of her husband. Her mother was happy. She couldn't dispute that.

"But what do you get out of this, Dad?"

He took a drag of his cigarette, blew the smoke into a cloud. It was cold enough that Kate's expelled breath was also visible. It mingled with the cigarette smoke, then disappeared.

"The first time I saw your mother was on a bus in downtown Philly," he said, his voice soft. "She was working at Mercy Hospital back then, and she was the most beautiful thing I'd ever seen.

"I didn't think she'd give a seventeen-year-old high-school dropout a second look so I told her I was twenty and talked her into meeting me for a drink. If I had it all to do over, I'd do the same thing. What she thinks of me matters. It always has."

Kate's fingers and toes and the tips of her ears were numb, but she stood rooted to the spot staring at her father instead of going back into the warmth of the house.

She'd decided long ago that her mother believed Dad's lies because Mom was the one in the relationship who loved more. She'd never considered that it might be the other way around.

"But I always thought Mom was the one who loved you more," she said.

"It's not like you can measure these things, Kate." Her dad dropped the cigarette butt and stamped out the embers. "If you'd ever been in love, you'd understand that."

But she was in love. With a man who'd said he loved her back.

Heavens, she was a fool. How could she have ever believed that love wasn't enough?

RILEY SAT IN THE buttery-soft leather sofa in his parents' family room, massaging the bridge of his nose and wondering how much more it would take to put him in the Christmas spirit.

He should have gotten jolly well before now.

Logs crackled in the fireplace, lights from the tree twinkled in the corner of the room and the air smelled of evergreen and candy cane-scented candles.

Mother had laid out a gourmet feast for Christmas Eve dinner, with sautéed duck with fresh asparagus and raspberry sauce as the centerpiece. But all Riley wanted was to put the season behind him.

He hadn't realized somebody had joined him until he saw brandy being thrust at him.

"I figured you needed this, squirt." His brother, Dave, sat down heavily beside him and stretched out his long legs.

Riley examined the amber liquid in the brandy snifter with skepticism. "Please tell me it's not apricot or cherry."

"Nope. No flavorings. It's from Dad's stash. I would have brought you a beer if there was any in the house."

Riley took a swig and let the warm liquid slide down his throat. "Where is Mom, anyway?"

"On the phone with Mrs. Dumont. Something about a cocktail party tomorrow afternoon."

"How soon can we leave without hurting her feelings?"

Dave checked the mahogany mantel clock and folded his hands behind his head. "Another hour at least. But we have to come back tomorrow. It's Christmas."

"Where's Dad?"

"She sent him out for more eggnog before the stores close."

Riley grimaced. "I hate eggnog."

"Me, too. I won't drink it, but I'm betting you'll choke down a glass to make her happy."

Riley put his untouched brandy snifter down on one of the coasters that protected the gleaming mahogany of the table. Brandy and eggnog didn't mix. "Mother's a hard woman to refuse."

"Then get ready for the Dumonts' cocktail party. I heard Mother tell Mrs. Dumont to be sure Elle was there because she planned to talk you into going."

Riley groaned and ran a hand over his face. "I don't know why she keeps pushing me and Elle together."

"Maybe because she doesn't know about Kate Marino. Why didn't you invite Kate over here for Christmas?"

Riley drew in a sharp breath at the sound of Kate's name, ruining his chance of pretending Dave hadn't hit a nerve. "Because she's in Philadelphia and thinking of staying there," Riley said gruffly.

Dave was silent for long moments before he said, "Ah, well. That's probably for the best. You've been hung up on her for too long. Maybe this'll make it easier for you to get over her."

"Maybe it won't," Riley snapped, appalled at his brother's comment. In no way could Kate leaving him be considered for the best. "I happen to be in love with her."

"Then why is she moving to Philadelphia?" Dave turned his head to peer at Riley. "Didn't you tell her you didn't want her to go?"

Riley didn't reply, but Dave must have read the answer on his face. "You know, for a smart guy, you sure can be an idiot," Dave said.

Riley slumped back against the sofa, his temper crackling along with the fire. So what if Dave never lacked for a date? That didn't mean he knew anything about women.

The silence between the brothers stretched for almost a minute before Riley couldn't take it any longer. "Okay, what did you mean by that crack?"

"Just that you've handled this all wrong, starting with that stupid plan to be her friend."

"It was not stupid," Riley said with heat.

"It didn't work, did it? You're here and she's there."

There wasn't much Riley could say to that, so he remained silent.

"Let me ask you something," Dave said, sitting up and turning toward him. "What did you say when she told you she might move?"

"I advised her to think it over carefully and do what was best for her."

"Idiot."

"Would you quit calling me that? I was trying to take things slow." Riley scowled at him. "What do you think I should have done?"

"Gone with your instincts. Told her you loved her. Said you couldn't live without her. Begged her not to go."

"I did tell her I loved her," he said, then thought about her puzzling parting comment about it not being enough. "But I'm not sure she believed me."

Dave got ready to say something else, but Riley cut him off. "Don't you dare call me an idiot again."

But maybe he was an idiot. The physical side of his relationship with Kate had progressed at warp speed, but he'd never actually laid out his feelings for her.

He slanted a look at his brother. "That stuff you said about going with my instincts—do you think that would have worked?"

"One way to find out." Dave reached for the clip on his belt, took off his cell phone and handed it to Riley. "I bet you won't have any problem getting a flight to Philly tomorrow. Planes are nearly empty on Christmas Day."

14

KATE DRAGGED HER SUITCASE into the foyer of her parents' house and took her Christmas-red coat from the hall closet. She dodged arms and shoulders as she shrugged into it, trying not to bump anyone else in the family, all of whom were also getting into their coats.

Christmas dinner at grandmother's house, which really was over the river and through the woods, was only an hour away.

"Johnny, would you go into the kitchen and get those loaves of Italian bread I picked up at the bakery?" her mother asked Kate's brother. "Oh, and the rest of the Italian fig cookies Kate and I baked."

"Sure Grandma won't get mad if you bring the cookies?" Johnny asked. "Remember that time you brought lasagna and she stuck it in the freezer?"

"That's because she prefers cooking her own Christmas lasagna," Kate reminded him. "She makes it with spinach so it'll be red and green."

Johnny made a face. "Gag me. I hate spinach."

"I love those cookies," her father interjected, helping her mother into her coat. "And if my mother yells at you, I'll yell back at her."

"You would not," her mother said, smiling tenderly at him. "You're too good a son to yell at your mother."

"Maybe so," he said, kissing her lightly on the lips, "but I'll think about doing it."

Kate picked up her suitcase, eager to get out of the house and put the day in motion. Because at the end of it, she'd be seeing Riley.

"You're sure you'll be able to break away and get me to the airport by five o'clock, right, Johnny?" she asked her brother when he came out of the kitchen with the bread and the cookies.

"Are you kidding? We're not at Grandma's yet and I already want to leave," he said, shaking his dark, too-long hair from his equally dark eyes.

"Your grandparents won't be happy about you leaving early, Kate," her father remarked.

"Maybe they'd accept it better, Frank, if you explained that Kate was going back to design the interior of a new resort hotel," her mother told him.

"I already did," Frank said.

"Did you tell them that the company hiring her is very prestigious?" her mom asked, then turned to Kate. "What was the name of it again, dear?"

"The Lowcountry Group," Kate said.

"I explained," her father said with a quirk of his eyebrows. "Your grandfather wants to know what kind of person calls and offers somebody a job on Christmas Eve and then expects them to start working on Christmas."

"I don't think Mr. Stein celebrates Christmas. And

I'm not actually going back early for the job," Kate said, thinking it might be time she told her family about Riley. "I'm going back for—"

The doorbell rang, cutting off her words. Everybody in the foyer froze, because nobody ever visited them on Christmas. The Marinos were the ones who did the visiting.

"I wonder who that could be." Her mother smoothed her hair and straightened her coat as she made the remark.

"Whoever it is, they'll get an eyeful of beautiful woman," her father told her with a wink, and she blushed before she pulled open the door to…

Riley? But could Riley really be here on her parents' doorstep, looking tall, dark and impossibly sexy? Kate blinked hard a few times, but he didn't vanish. His eyes warmed when they met hers, but then he looked around at the curious faces staring back at him.

"Who are you?" her father asked.

Kate cleared her throat to unfreeze her vocal chords, and said, "This is Riley Carter, my…friend from Charleston."

Kate was fairly certain that Riley grimaced at the description, but she plowed ahead with the introductions after he came into the house. Then she suffered through the handshakes and polite words when all she really wanted was to find out what Riley was doing here.

When everybody knew who everybody else was, her mother's gaze panned from Riley to Kate and then back again. "So the two of you are *friends?*"

"Actually," Riley said, not taking his eyes from Kate, "that's what I'm here to talk to her about."

What did that mean? Kate wondered as her pulse spiked, her palms grew damp and her breathing snagged.

"What does that mean?" her father piped in. "Are you her friend or aren't you? Because we're on our way to Christmas dinner at her grandparents'. So if you are her friend, I'd invite you along, but if you're not—"

"Frank," her mother interrupted, tugging on his arm, "I think that means we should leave them alone."

"But then Kate will miss dinner," her father protested.

"Can I miss dinner?" Johnny asked.

Riley gestured to a parked American-made sedan at the curb. "I have a rental car, Mr. Marino. I'll be glad to drive your daughter there."

"But—"

"Let's go, Frank," her mother insisted, practically yanking him and Johnny out the door, stopping only long enough to tell Riley it was nice to have met him.

And then Kate and Riley were alone.

He shoved both his hands into the pockets of his brown leather bomber jacket, letting his eyes roam over her. She felt his gaze as though it were a torch. "You sure do look pretty today, Kate."

His predilection for not getting straight to the point had never been more maddening. "What did you mean about wanting to talk to me about us being friends?"

He ran a hand over his brow, then raised his eyes to the ceiling, from which a sprig of mistletoe hung. "Ah, hell," he said, and swept her into his arms. Before she had time to process what was happening, his mouth was on hers, hot and demanding and passionate.

She kissed him back, a little desperately because she'd thought she might never kiss him again. But this kiss was different from the others they'd shared, because this time she didn't try to hold back the love she'd always felt for him. It poured out of her, thick and hot and festive.

The kiss went on and on, making her knees weak, making her heart full, making her feel as though she might roast because she was still wearing her coat. And then he drew back, staring at her with as bemused an expression as she was sure must be on her own face.

"What was that?" she whispered.

"That was me acting on my impulses."

She smiled. "I like it."

"I love you," he said, his eyes dark and intense. "I like you, too. But I loved you before I liked you, which isn't the way I thought it was supposed to happen. That's why I came up with the plan to be your friend.

"I was going to take it slow, the way I thought I should have taken it the first time we were together. But I couldn't, because I love you too damn much. And now I think maybe we weren't meant to go slow. Maybe you and me, we're on the fast track."

She blinked tears of happiness from her eyes, but found she could tease him. "For a slow-talking guy, that sure was a mouthful."

"There's more I want to say. I don't want to live without you, Kate," he said, and she read the truth in his eyes, where she now thought it had always been. "I want to marry you, Kate. I want to spend my life with you."

"Then why did you ask me to live with you?"

"Because I didn't want to ruin things by rushing you into anything." He rolled his eyes. "And here I am in your parents' house about to offer to move to Philadelphia."

"You'd move to Philadelphia for me?" she asked, stunned.

When he stroked her cheek, his fingers shook, just slightly but enough that she noticed. "I'd do anything for you."

She turned her face and kissed the tips of his fingers. "Then will you stay in Charleston?" At his puzzled expression, she continued, "Because the Lowcountry Group offered me a job remodeling a hotel in North Charleston. Turned out, they liked my modern interiors so much, they thought of me for the job right away."

Riley's eyes lit up as brightly as any Christmas light. "That's great. It's exactly what you wanted." His expression changed, grew more serious. "But that's why you're going back to Charleston, isn't it? It's not because of me."

She gestured to her suitcase, which was still beside the door. "I have a five o'clock flight, Riley. I couldn't wait any longer to find you and make you listen to me."

"About what?" He sounded hopeful and skeptical at the same time.

"About this theory I used to have about relationships. I thought there always had to be one person who loved the other more."

"In our case, that'd be me," Riley said. "No. Don't interrupt. There's something I've got to say. I never did tell you why I didn't move away when Elle kissed me."

"It's not important," she muttered.

"It is. It was an experiment. I was afraid, Kate. Afraid of how fast things were moving between us. I wanted to see if I'd feel the same when I kissed somebody else as I did when I kissed you. But it wasn't even close."

"So you're saying you kissed her because you were in love with me?"

He nodded.

"But I broke up with you because I was afraid I loved you too much." She shook her head at the mess she'd made. "I always knew in my heart you didn't cheat on me. But it was easier to let you believe that than it was to take a chance."

"I'm not sure I follow," Riley said, touching her hair, her cheeks, her mouth.

"It's a long story. I'll tell it to you someday," she said. "But all you need to know for now is that, since I came back to Philly, I learned that you can't quantify love."

"But if you could," he said, "I'd be the one who loves more."

"I don't know about that." She stood on her tiptoes and put her heart into her kiss. When she was through, she asked, "What do you think now?"

"I think the answer's inconclusive, but I'm willing to keep experimenting," he said, and dipped his head for another kiss.

introduces an exciting new family saga with

DYNASTIES : THE DANFORTHS

A family of prominence...
tested by scandal, sustained by passion!